J'Nita's Family Tree

R.S. Brown

Order this book online at www.trafford.com
or email orders@trafford.com

Most Trafford titles are also available at major online book retailers.

Note for Librarians: A cataloguing record for this book is available from Library
and Archives Canada at www.collectionscanada.ca/amicus/index-e.html

Printed in Victoria, BC, Canada.

ISBN: 978-1-4269-0781-4 (sc)

*We at Trafford believe that it is the responsibility of us all, as both individuals
and corporations, to make choices that are environmentally and socially sound.
You, in turn, are supporting this responsible conduct each time you purchase a
Trafford book, or make use of our publishing services. To find out how you are
helping, please visit www.trafford.com/responsiblepublishing.html*

*Our mission is to efficiently provide the world's finest, most comprehensive
book publishing service, enabling every author to experience success.
To find out how to publish your book, your way, and have it available
worldwide, visit us online at www.trafford.com*

 www.trafford.com

North America & international
toll-free: 1 888 232 4444 (USA & Canada)
phone: 250 383 6864 ♦ fax: 812 355 4082

For my Family, especially my mother and father, John and Helen, my sons, Sean, Yale and Adam, my sister, Nina, and my brother, Matthew.

I thank God for the inspiration and patience

Contents

Preface

Preface

It has been nearly three decades since Alex Haley wrote <u>Roots</u> and impacted the public, especially African-Americans, with the notion about discovering kinship and learning about the past. <u>J'Nita's Family Tree</u> is a story about characters who are eager to learn who their ancestors were, where they were from and what they were like. The story depicts a different journey of discovery than <u>Roots,</u> but it verifies the genre in other intriguing ways that makes it unique. It expands the historical significance of the genre, that is, the search for kinship. During the 20th century, there were more inquiries about tracing ancestry than any time. Millions of people have poured through records and archives and have met with success like the characters in <u>J'Nita's Family Tree</u>. The investigation is rewarding when a discovery yields confirmation of who you are and where you are from.

The computer and technology make it easier for discovery where a simple DNA test or a data entry item can result in a link to the past more readily than we ever thought possible and with a high degree of accuracy. Whichever way one traces kinship and the past, it can result in a revelatory and enriching experience by learning who we are. Histories are made, talked about and investigated. It is worthwhile research to learn about the past as there are many, many more stories to explore.

The Author

Chapter 1

Grandma's Home-going

Swing Low, swing chariot
Coming for to carry me home
Swing low, swing chariot
Coming for to carry me home.

The wooden coffin was carried out of the church by the pallbearers with the spiritual chiming from the belfry. Everyone walked somberly through the double doors of the church and onto the streets where groups of people congregated waiting to see the last rites bestowed upon the deceased. The coffin was cumbersomely put into the hearse, the door shut and the crowd watched the procession begin to the burial ground. Some of the people followed in their cars and others went their separate ways with memories of the funeral of Amalya's grandmother.

Death had come to Amalya and her family. Their maternal grandmother had died and Amalya still felt the anguish in every fiber and nerve from the moment she learned about her grandmother's death. The image of her lifeless body would not vanish as she rode morbidly silent to the cemetery. It was not that her grandmother's death was unexpected. Her grandmother was nearly a hundred years old when she passed. That was a long time to live, nearly a century. The world had changed drastically: wars had taken place; children had become adults; and she, Amalya had married and had a child. Her grandmother's death was difficult for her to come to terms with because she had raised her; had been her mother, father and grandparent when her mother died. The passing of Grandma's daughter, Amalya's mother, had been immensely difficult but Grandma made certain that Amalya had everything she had hoped for her daughter and. reassured Amalya that she would be around for as long as God allowed.

Longevity had its stay with Grandma. Grandma's endurance was legend. It was like she was at the helm steering a long and great marathon which was why Amalya was having difficulty coming to terms with her death - Grandma had been pervasive throughout her life and she had come to expect her presence. Seeing Grandma's lifeless body in the midst of the obsequy, Amalya realized now that any day would have been unexpected. Those thoughts lingered into the well of her sorrow for she knew she would never see Grandma again or hear her encouraging words.

Suddenly, Amalya felt the nudge of her daughter, J'Nita, putting her head on her shoulder. She was proud of her daughter's reserve and understanding about what had taken place. J'Nita was sorrowful the moment she heard that Grandma had died but assumed an aura of maturity and acceptance: "I will miss Grandma," she commented with downcast eyes as if she did not want her mother to see her tears. J'Nita was very much like her, Amalya thought.

As they rode, Amalya remembered the times they had visited Grandma's. Grandma lived less than fifteen miles from them and it was always a pleasant trip they looked forward to like going to a much needed retreat. On a carved out road that had recently been constructed to connect the back wooded areas to the commercial areas, Amalya and J'Nita would ride as early in the morning as they were able to gather their things to take with them on their visit.

Along the way, the once dense forest was divided with a road that made towns more accessible to travelers and long time residents take notice of the steady stream of traffic they had never seen before and reminding them of the signaled change. Concession stands with brightly colored billboards of fruits and vegetables were erected and scattered approximate miles apart. They enjoyed stopping at one particular concession to browse, inspect and eventually buy some produced: greens, melons, tomatoes or some other fresh vegetable or fruit they favored before proceeding to Grandma's.

Grandma would always hear and see them arrive; she would walk out of the house and stand at the gatepost and wait for them to step out of the car. Then, together they would either walk around the yard and grounds and inspect the garden and verdure or go directly to the kitchen and settle. The aromas of fresh apple cider and raisin biscuits lured Amalya into feeling that moment was reality and not what was taking place. She could still taste the savory treats and hear Grandma's voice apologizing for not inviting them to a special gathering she had attended. It was not until the limousine made a turn onto the road leading to the burial ground that she looked out of the window to see continuous plots of graves, flowers, crosses and vaults.

Amalya repelled at the images that eradicated her former visions and resisted what would inevitably take place.   Instead, she heard her Grandmother's conciliatory voice explaining one of the last moments she spent with her friend: "I didn't mean to forget you, but Mrs. Carlton was here before I had time to think. She was having a celebration for her son who had returned from the army.   I was astonished and quite certain I wanted to attend.   I prepared myself immediately. She was here the minute I looked up. I was in high anticipation to see him in uniform because you know, I remembered him as a baby. Brian Carlton is now a man of the world. He has seen places I can't imagine. That is what this world is becoming for you youngsters, a big, open universe. The Carlton's were fortunate to have Brian return from the war."   The memory warmed the voided space in Amalya about her Grandmother and the veneration she always felt for her grandmother pervaded.

Grandma was so vital that day, Amalya thought, what had she missed in Grandma's manner or conversation that would have given her a clue. Amalya agonized over what she could not explain or understand.   The procession was slowing and she became more resistance. The memories of Grandma's last day were more compelling. …

The day at the office was routine, but at some point she received word of a phone call. She was somewhat concerned as to who it might be as she walked from the clamoring work space.   Was it Garland, her husband; she became slightly alarmed; maybe it was Grandma or J'Nita, the school, or a business call.

She was alarmed when she lifted the receiver and heard Mrs. Carlton's voice. Why, she wondered, why was Mrs. Carlton calling? She listened.

"Amalya, you near a place where there's a chair? If you are, sit in it, honey and gather your strength 'cause this isn't something you want to hear. God knows, I didn't want to be the one to tell you this, but your Grandma's gone. I just decided to pay her a visit today and, well, you can imagine. I can't put it into words. You there, Amalya? You listening?"

Every word reverberated. Panic and disbelief arose, even hurt and sorrow in case it was true. Grandma's dead? No, it couldn't be, thought Amalya as she abruptly hung up the phone. She had just visited Grandma last evening. Besides, it was not what she had envisioned in her most courageous thoughts or scenarios in case, if and when something should happen to Grandma. This was another circumstance and completely unlike what she had imagined with tributary, last words and acceptance. If it had been anyone other than Mrs. Carlton, she might have thought it a cruel prank. She had to know; she had to find out for certain. She moved anxiously. Unaware of how she might be perceived, she informed her supervisor and left immediately.

The news about Grandma rested heavily upon her as she drove. A whir of visions and thoughts began to assert: "Mrs. Carlton is probably right. She is more knowledgeable about things than she is," thought Amalya. Regardless, Amalya did not want her Grandma to be dead. She felt an emptiness; no explanation could ease her burden of knowing.

When she turned onto the road leading to Grandma's house, a dark cloud surrounded her like a fear she had never known. It was probably true –

Grandma was dead. The thought echoed louder and louder and she felt dreadful and if she budged, her whole world would come crashing down and something uncontrollable might happen. With caution from within, she exerted all of her strength to avoid a catastrophe. Seeing the house come into view, she would now confront the truth. Was Mrs. Carlton certain? She hoped it wasn't true.

She stopped the car directly in front of the house. The white light of the afternoon made the green trim encased windows glare from the refracting rays of sun. The scintillate glow revived in Amalya the many summers she immersed herself in embryonic childhood, as Grandma imposed her stature and guarded her like a sentinel.

In the distance, she could see the houses of the neighbors and nearby community. Had word about Grandma reached them, she wondered as she stepped out of the car. The colorful luster of autumn abound, reminding her of the coming season. She began to move deliberately, as if not to forestall another moment about the mystery surrounding her grandmother.

Soon, she stood at the front door scrutinizing the six windowpanes revealing white voile curtains on the other side. They were the same yesterday, she noted. She turned the knob of the door and opened it. Seeing Dr. Ryan and Mrs. .Carlton in the foyer instead of Grandma, and a strange feeling of doom overpowered her. She did not have a second to think or talk, only to listen to Dr. Ryan explain, without hesitation, that Grandma had died. The truth brought a sad weariness of mind and limb. After informing Amalya about Grandma, Dr. Ryan next escorted her to where her body lay. She cast her eyes on Grandma's still body and thought: "She looks to be asleep, Dr. Ryan, are you certain?" Those words never rose above a whisper. Once Amalya acknowledged that Grandma was no longer alive, Dr. Ryan took a white muslin sheet and shrouded her body. Mrs. Carlton was consoling as this happened: "Your Grandma was quite a person and was blessed to live a long time, but humans are mortals and all of us will realize that one day." …

Dr. Ryan closed his black medicine bag and clutched the handles to carry with him when he left. Over the years, he had become known as the doctor who made house calls and carried such a heavy medicine bag that it made his body sag to one side. "The undertaker is on its way," he informed Amalya.

Death carries a barrier between it and the world until it happens. From the time Grandma was pronounced dead and was carried from the house, it – death – was pervasive; pitiful; strange; and unnatural to the human condition. Amalya could neither deny nor accept what had happened. Her eyes followed each act and minute detail devoid of thought and feeling. It was not until she had to inform J'Nita that words found meaning and then the tightness and lump that had formed and stifled her speech, disintegrated and raspy, harsh words escaped about what had happened to Grandma. She realized how difficult it must have been for Mrs. Carlton to inform her because it was nearly impossible for her to relate the fact about Grandma's death to J'Nita: "Things happen that are beyond our control," were the words expressed by Amalya and made final the unexpected truth. At least she was able to speak, but still unable to comprehend.

Amalya looked up and saw Garland waiting to help them out of the limousine.

"Take your time. I know how difficult this is for you," he commented. Amalya didn't know how long he was waiting. She only knew she did not want to climb out of the limousine and join the procession to the grave. At the moment, the only thing that held her together was J'Nita and suddenly a source of strength propelled her forward. Garland took her arm consolingly. "It'll be alright," he reassured her.

There was a chill in the air, the kind that made for discomfort and reminded Amalya that she didn't want to be where she was for the reason that was intended. She saw the canopy where they would sit under or stand under until the obsequies were finished. She saw the Carlton's and her friends and that made her feel the final ceremony was important to them also. There seats were reserved in front of the casket and when they arrived they sat in them. The casket was draped with white satin and purple embroidered cross. Amalya was distance; she didn't see or meet anyone's eyes, but felt them hovering and waiting to be sent back into the world of the living. The minister began, but she didn't hear him at first. When he began Psalm 23, she heard.

The Lord is my shepherd, I shall not want;

Grandmother loved that psalm, she thought. She even memorized it. Throughout her life she had repeated some of words for whatever reason, the words just came to her and it seemed appropriate for her to repeat. Now the entire psalm was being sung.

He maketh me to lie down in green pastures; he leadeth me beside still waters

Amalya listened intently. What Grandma would do to hear that psalm; thus, in her way she was listening for the both of them.

He restoreth my soul: he leadeth me in the paths of righteousness for his name's sake.

Amalya understood her grandmother more now than ever. In a way, it was not pity or tragedy but something more glorious than she could describe; the words spoke for her life and her death.

Yea, though I walk through the valley of the shadow of death, I will fear no evil; for thou art with me; they rod and they staff they comfort me.
She realized that her Grandma left the earth doing what she liked best and being with those she loved most.

Thou preparest a table before me in the presence of mine enemies; thou anointest my head with oil; my cup runneth over.

Amalya was glad they walked the gardens and grounds around the house the last day she saw her. Everything was so carefully planted and set. Gardening was one of Grandma's greatest joys.

Surely goodness and mercy shall follow me all the days of my life; and I will dwell in the house of the Lord forever.

For as long as her life allowed, Amalya promised to keep the gardens and grounds just like Grandma had.

Ashes to ashes, Dust to dust …

Amalya stood firm in her commitment as she placed a flower on the coffin and bid farewell to her Grandma.

***

At least a week had passed since her Grandma's burial. Amalya had the arduous task of writing thank you notes to those who attended. Amalya had attempted the task many times before but was not able to follow through. So many friends and family had attended and now she was reminded it was imperative to thank them for attending her grandmother's home going. She felt something urging her to go beyond; to see through the difficulties of adjusting to her Grandma's absence. What happened was both extraordinary and ordinary. She could not forget Grandma in just one day. It would probably take her life time; so she had to get used to it, she reminded herself. Even though she was daunted, she rose above every possible resistance within her and began to write the first thank you note. She saw the many well wishers and not her anguish and it was all the better because she wrote what was necessary to say to them for the occasion.

From time to time she looked through the window of the quaint and cozy room to see autumn in full bloom. It was dark and colorful with just enough light for her to finish writing the thank you notes. Everything reminded her of Grandma, like her spirit was there reminding her of what she had to do. It is said that the spirit lives on. Amalya drew comfort knowing that Grandma in some way was still vital. Names were written in the salutation, words were composed appropriate for the occasion. She tried to remember some of the faces and what they said to console her: "Your grandmother lived a long time. What a nice person. She was blessed, truly blessed. We're sorry to hear about your grandmother." It was like she was reliving the ceremony. They were defining her grandmother and she was trying to convey those thoughts also by way of gratitude. The time she spent made it possible for her to remember her grandmother in a different way. She began to understand she really did love and understand her and she relished all that her grandmother intended. She was more certain now of what she needed to say for there are no words better expressed after death that brings meaning to life.* When she checked the cards remaining, there were only four left. She had intentionally put aside those for her friends. She breathed a sigh of relief like a burden had been lifted. This is what is done. It is part of the obsequy. Life is sometimes simple and more complicated than we care to unravel, but that burden was vanquished, she acceded.

She looked at the remaining cards to be completed. Those were for her friends. They had known each other since childhood and had done everything together like friends do. She could not remember a day being without one or the other of her friends. Neither could she really decide who her best friend was. Before they knew the full intent and purpose of the word *bond*, they had vowed to be there for each other. When they heard that grandma passed, they quickly came to her side to form a protective shield in case anything should happen to her. They were like her thoughts and actions during the ordeal. Her friend, Alana, presently came to mind, if for no other reason than she met her in the fifth grade, sat side by side, announced their names and a long friendship ensued. Year after year, they were like each other's shadow, everything similar: the same progress, the same pain and pleasure, the same achievement, and they even had daughters around the same age who were also friends. When Alana received the card, thought Amalya, she would be the first to say "Amalya didn't have to write any thank you note," ... but if she had forgotten, she would have reminded her in some cryptic way. In any event, Amalya could not forget her genuine concern when Alana offered to be present at the obsequies – those formalities and morbid details for placing a soul in its final resting place. "You need someone with you," Alana insisted. Amalya did not protest for it was a very dark order and gathering in her mind with nothing familiar or embracing.

Without further delay or difficulty, she composed some formal thoughts to Alana. Appropriate words flowed as easily as their frequent conversations. They had shared many intimate things; their likes, fears and troubles and still they had mundane things to talk and laugh about. She expressed appreciation in diverse ways, beginning with: "Friends understand these difficult moments and make things easier to bear," etc. She wrote until she was certain Alana would "read between the lines," as they would always say as a final note to what they were trying to convey. She then folded the card and placed it in the envelope. She stood up, walked around the room again, but mindful not to leave because she had to complete the task and was now more driven to do so. Then, well ... she knew what was next ... ritual and duty ... another drive to Grandma's, but under different circumstances.

She looked through the window into the night and noticed a peace had settled in the sky. Glittering stars like myriad of lights cast around the moon. In time, everything will be completed, the thought crossed her mind. A preoccupation: the war had ended; she had wanted it to end. ... Tomorrow? Amalya began to organize everything that she had to do regarding her grandmother. Garland, her husband, would not be home for at least a couple of days; he worked for the railroad and traveled long distances. Perfect, she reasoned. She and J'Nita would drive to Grandma's and ... well, whatever happens, whatever they had to do. ... It was settled.

The inquiring voice of J'Nita intruded as she walked briskly into the room.

"Are you all right, Mama," she wanted to know.

"I'll be just fine, what about you?"

"I was thinking about Grandma. I was thinking about her because I miss her," J'Nita admitted somberly.

"I know what you mean, that's only natural," Amalya assured her as she escorted J'Nita towards the divan. "Sit down, honey," she offered. J'Nita followed and both of them sat on the divan.

"You know, Grandma used to enjoy being in this room. Both of us miss her because she was so much a part of our lives, but in time we'll reach an understanding and we will be able to cherish the memories we have of her. If it helps, remember Grandma was a strong and proud person, and a person like that would want anyone close to her to stand in the face of adversity with dignity and grace. That would really make her proud, and to begin our recovery, tomorrow we're going to visit Grandma's."

"Go back to the cemetery," questioned J'Nita.

"No, no, we're going to drive over to Grandma's house."

"Grandma's not there anymore," reminded J'Nita.

"I know, but there are things that must be done because she isn't there anymore and I want you to go with me. Do you think you're up to it?"

"Sure, Mama, I always like visiting Grandma's," J'Nita replied eagerly.

"Fine, you get your rest because tomorrow, we're going to start real early for our trip to Grandma's. Okay?"

"Okay," J'Nita agreed and arose from the divan, embraced her mother and walked out of the room.

Amalya returned to the table to finish the thank you notes that remained. She thought about Grandma and she thought about J'Nita's reaction when she told her that Grandma had passed. . For over a decade, their generations had co-existed. Grandma had ample influence on both of them. Grandma was like their anchor who secured them in their uncertainty. Amalya will always remember her Grandma telling her: "The labor of a child does not end after birth." Certainly, Amalya gradually understood what her Grandma meant as J'Nita grew. In her most difficult moments, Grandma was there to reassure her. Grandma's special wisdom transcended Amalya's understanding when J'Nita became very ill one day causing Amalya to be in a panic and at a lost what to do because it was one of the few times Dr. Ryan could not be contacted. J'Nita's condition seemed to worsen every second Amalya waited to get medical attention and grew in proportion to her fears. The feverish, trembling body of J'Nita pressed against her in whines and whimpers. Amalya had desperate hope that J'Nita's condition would subside quickly, but when it didn't, she called Grandma.

When Grandma saw J'Nita writhing in pain, she was calm and consoling and, within a short time, restored reason to the situation. "Amalya, I see you're overwhelmed by this. J'Nita is suffering through spasmodic episodes, but she'll be all right in the morning. Get yourself some rest in the meantime." The next morning, J'Nita's prognosis was good and she appeared normal and energetic as Grandma proudly held J'Nita to show her health was restored.

Amalya was tearful but grateful to Grandma for everything she had done for her and J'Nita. She realized it would take a long time for the memories of Grandma to recede. Her unyielding determination made her return to the task of finishing the thank you notes.

Seeing the name of Ophelia made her concern about Ophelia return. She sat recollecting what they had discussed before she received the phone call about Grandma. It was not a routine conversation, she remembered. She ruminated until the conversation they had was prominent in her mind. Ophelia was considering moving from the area. Amalya's reaction was that of bewilderment. "Move, Ophelia, where?"

"Florida or Atlanta or maybe even one of the big cities, New York or Chicago, I'm not sure yet," Ophelia responded. Amalya was careful not to encourage her decision one way or the other because she didn't want to see her leave and disrupt their circle of togetherness and friendship. Amalya was relieved when she was informed that she had a call and hurriedly ended the conversation: "You can't leave. I'll talk to you about it later, I have a call."

Things had changed since then. She really wanted to resume their conversation, and thought of calling her, but wrote some ornate words instead: "In times like these, friends really understand." ... It wasn't all she wanted to say, but other words were inappropriate. They *would* talk later, she decided as she sealed the card.

Amalya had persistent thoughts about Ophelia. She was proving to be an unconventional woman. She had not married and settled down when everyone else did. But, she was her best defense about the subject: "There isn't anything wrong. You look at what's going on, the war, the anger and unrest, and I consider myself to be in good shape. I'm fine inside of me. The war has to end and people have to come to some real understanding. Amalya had overlooked most things about Ophelia thinking maybe one day the rest of them would look up and she would be married also. Now, she was reconsidering some things about her. Like war changed Ophelia, death had changed her views and feelings. What was really important? ... Some people are not conventional in the way you expect. Move? Stay? Amalya could not decide how to convince Ophelia.

Two cards were left to write: one for Elisha and the other for Renee. When they heard about Grandma, they treated her as delicate as a flower fearing she would wither away. They spoke few words beyond sympathetic ones, but were present the entire time. Amalya wrote: Dear Elisha ... Dear Renee ... one card superimposed on the other: *Serenity,* and those words that go with serenity were spelled out along with *Acceptance*. It was all she could bear to write. All of them would talk about the matter many times until it faded in time and memory. The task of writing the cards ended with a long sigh from Amalya. She stamped them and piled them neatly for mailing.

Emptiness like night and hunger followed momentarily. Beyond that was Grandma's house: vacant, quiet, all the people gone and matters were left in mystery. She began to survey the house in her mind. She knew every room and corner from the clock on the mantle in the living room to the creaking rocking chairs in the attic. How to regard things when she arrived tomorrow proposed: separate, remove, make useful again. Her mind went in orderly fashion for the next task. She had to persevere. J'Nita would be with her and she wanted to show determination and courage as Grandma would have expected her to do. Grandma's shrouded body flashed; unforgettable like the moment she saw it. Amalya did all she could to rid the image as it made her sorrowful once again.

She prompted herself to prepare for tomorrow. She had the rest of the evening to do what was necessary. She took the stack of cards and placed them on the mahogany table by the door where they would be visible and she would not forget to mail them when they left in the morning. She looked forward to going to Grandma's.

Her life seemed to resuscitate. She thought about Garland. He was always her first and last thoughts when he was away. She imagined him staring at her from some city or town he had arrived. He had been around the country and had seen most of the states. He was knowledgeable and could relate cities, towns, even lakes and rivers like one who had learned another language. Many evenings, he would lull her to sleep with stories about the places had had been. He had even invited her and J'Nita to Florida. J'Nita enjoyed Disney World and basked in the excitement and sunny weather. Amalya seemed to hear the mighty roar of the train and yearned for one fascinating story of faraway places from Garland, but was resigned to wait until he returned.

She glanced at her image as she wrapped a scarf around the carefully set rollers. She stared in thought about the several days she spent in tribulation. Sleep only came through desperation and then it was not restful, but a continuum of what was taking place: death, ritual, people, and emotions exuding everywhere. Tonight might be different, she thought. Rest will be peaceful and she would wake up renewed. She wished Garland were home to reassure her like he had when he first heard about Grandma's death. Amalya was able to contact him through the Railway System, and within a day, his schedule was interrupted and he returned home. Clad in uniform: a pale blue shirt and dark trousers, he embraced and consoled her. "Your Grandma's spirit lives on." Garland understood what Grandma meant to her.

From the beginning, experience and intuition convinced Grandma that they were meant for each other. My husband, your Grandpa, died long ago, but I believe Garland will always be there for you. Grandma was right, Amalya realized. She was anxious for his safe return from his trip. Amalya began to hum the song played at the funeral:

Swing Low, swing chariot
Coming for to carry me home
Swing low, swing chariot
Coming for to carry me home.

The events of the funeral recurred before she slept. Other than her friends, she really didn't recognize anyone, but she knew they were from the community;

they knew Grandma and her family. She probably met with them and spoke with them, but during that time she didn't recognize them, now she understood why. An uncontrollable sadness possessed her that was overwhelming and she only wanted to sleep so that she might not feel the anguish.

Sleep was more like dream in the darkened night. Amalya was compelled to see images and visions. She didn't know what to make of what she saw but she was like one seeing the horizon for the first time. She wanted to comprehend; to perceive what surrounded her. Some faces seemed familiar but she wasn't sure. Suddenly she felt herself being twirled freely and others around her were moving similarly, happily carefree and dancing around an invisibly drawn circle. When it seemed they had completed the circle, an elderly man and woman silenced the crowd to a murmur: "Like the beginning and end, we are the first and you are the next. May you stand here one day and embrace another generation. Go and find yourselves back here one day." The crowd dispersed in a cheering roar. Out of the chaos, a change evolved. Amalya felt abandoned. There was desolation and dread. She wanted to leave. Desperation daunted her. Her strength waned in trepidation. "Grandma," she uttered aloud as she always had whenever she was in fear. To Amalya's amazement, Grandma appeared with a large and weighty book, larger than her entire body and the space she stood, it seemed to overpower her so that Amalya could not see her face only the book and the sound of her voice. "I give this to you; this is about our family," she offered. "I must leave now, Amalya, but I offer this to you."

"Grandma," Amalya called in desperation, but Grandma had already disappeared.

.

Chapter 2

Into the Past

Grandma's spirit does live on," Amalya realized as she awakened. "Today is the tomorrow I looked forward to," she thought as she donned her robe. There is much to be done at Grandma's. The dream about Grandma was still prevalent in her mind and lingered in its portent causing her to reflect upon a meaning. She envisioned Grandma's house once again; maybe there is such a book, she pondered and vowed to regard everything like an archaeological discovery.

She walked down the hall to J'Nita's room and was greeted with: "I can't wait to go to Grandma's. What if Grandma has some valuable treasures stored away?" J'Nita had awakened before dawn and prepared to accompany her mother to Grandma's. She had already dressed and was anxiously waiting for her mother. Many thoughts had occurred in the meantime pertaining to her fears; she knew it would be unnatural and even mysterious for them to walk into Grandma's house and not see her like they always had; that was the greatest barrier she had thought and thought about; as she could not imagine not having her grandmother present.

"Searching through the past will certainly have its rewards. We have much to accomplish today, and we have been blessed with clear weather. We'll leave after breakfast," her mother informed.

They moved hurriedly as they were consumed by the challenge ahead. They could only imagine what to expect as the void of Grandma's absence began to assert its influence within them. They knew that in less than two weeks their world had changed. The unknown had visited them and changed their view of life substantially. There was a burden like never before. They had not gotten used to what had happened and that was the problem – how to get used to what had happened. Both of them began to replace what was missing with optimism and talked incessantly about what they could expect to accomplish at Grandma's. In between spoonfuls of cereal and sips of coffee, they lay out their plans for the day. They imagined themselves as courageous women blazing an uncommon trail.

"Now you know what we have to do and what we have to remember," commented Amalya.

"Yes, of course. Grandma would have wanted us to conduct things as if she were here guiding us," said J'Nita.

J'Nita quickly finished her cereal and then joined her mother in clearing away the breakfast dishes.

"We're on our way now," Amalya announced in avid anticipation. The idea of exploration made the prospect of going to Grandma's more exciting. Inundated with possibilities and mysteries, Amalya was steadily ordering how things would be accomplished as J'nita listened intently. Incredibly, the burden of mourning was beginning to abate; the darkness of tragedy and sorrow was lifting With the last utensil put away, both of them left the kitchen.

Amalya took the stack of thank you cards with her as she and J'Nita left the house. She made one stop to the mailbox to deposit the cards and then proceeded directly to Grandma's.

The wide tract of land was before her; she looked at the earth: red, yellow, orange and gold; bright prisms of colors in motion, everywhere was picturesque and in season. Grandma's house lay beyond, the rooms set with items in place, at least Amalya remembered them being in place the last time she was there, as Grandma's lifeless body was carried away, but Amalya was determined not to be impeded by anything. It was part of life – death, but she had not yet come to terms. In time, she thought.   She noticed J'Nita looking inquisitively, but she had not voiced any questions or concerns. Amalya realized both of them in their own way were preparing for what they might find at Grandma's.   It would be profoundly different, but Amalya thought she understood the situation well enough to follow through.

Early morning made the drive seem a stone's throw away. At a distance, Amalya could see the concession stand with wooden crates and billboard signs of fruits and vegetables. This time, she had seen it right away, but it was not yet opened. Even if it were open, she would not have stopped. It would be a while before she approached it again because it reminded her of Grandma.

Amalya made a sharp right turn onto the road where the house was. Suddenly and unexpectedly, she felt herself go limp as the house came into view. "This is what happens, it is a normal reaction," she perceived, as if someone was speaking to her from a remote place which caused her to repossess herself again. The fear had subsided when she drove in front of the house.

"We're here," J'Nita exclaimed. "I can't wait to go inside, can you?"

"I think we can look forward to an interesting day," commented Amalya.

Before entering the house, they surveyed the grounds. Amalya observed the tree like one suddenly struck by the presence of grandeur. All elements meshed in one, the beauty of nature, the passing of time and the advent of another season. It reminded her of the dream, its presence more significant than she could readily understand; she remained in awe of its portent.

"I can't climb that tree anymore," J'Nita complained.

That's a mighty tree; you climbed as far as you could," Amalya encouraged.

"You think so," J'Nita wondered.

"Of course, look at it," suggested Amalya.

Both of them stood admiring the dense oak tree with bright colors making it look more magnificent. Finally, Amalya prompted: "We shouldn't waste another second." Both of them turned from the tree and walked towards the house.

Standing at the door, Amalya suddenly remembered no one was there to open it. She fumbled and searched for the key and when she found it, she looked at it strangely before using it to open the door for it reminded her of a world that had suddenly vanished. Now, she was uncertain what she would find. When she finally unlocked the door and opened it, they heard the clock on the mantle chiming as they entered. Amalya was startled and J'Nita fascinated.

"Grandma's clock still works," said J'Nita. Amalya nodded as she checked the time: 7:00 A.M. just early enough, she thought. They had much to accomplish and the day would probably go by quickly. The last chime ended and an eerie silence prevailed. J'Nita followed Amalya from room to room curiously.

Everything was still in place as Grandma had last seen things. Amalya glanced around the living room with sofa, chairs, tables and lamps and knick-knacks; then she peered at the adjoining dining room so formal and orderly with four chairs set under a finished wooden table, silver revere bowl with waxed fruit sat atop an oblong doily, and matching china and buffet cabinets. She remembered countless days spent in these favorite meeting places with family and friends, and she recalled some of the occasions as she studied the items in the rooms: the pictures of family in frames, the books and magazines; the vases now with withered flowers Grandma had carefully arranged before she passed; she loved fresh flowers from the garden. The floral fragrance lingered in the rooms.

After reasonable scrutiny, they proceeded to the kitchen and pantry. They did not remain very long because it was apparent Grandma had not gotten as far as those rooms the day she died. The next room, a day room, was as far as she had gotten; she probably entered from the outer hall. The door to that room remained closed. Amalya gave long and hard thought as to whether they should enter it. Something within her resisted. She could not bear the appearance of Grandma being wheeled away covered with white sheet and lifeless. Mrs. Carlton had prepared her that day: "Amalya, if this is your first time experiencing death, it's not very pleasant. I know how close you and your Grandma were. If you can't bear it, it's understandable." Amalya reassured Mrs. Carlton that she could face up to it, but in reality, it was a greater burden than she had ever experienced. They walked pass that room and directly to the stairs leading to the second floor. As they proceeded, Amalya took account of what was there.

At the top of the stairs, Amalya first saw in the hall, the commode with mirror above it. The doors to the rooms were opened; three in all: Grandma's room, her room and the guest room. After briefly peering in each room and seeing everything was in place: bed made, curtains pulled back with light shining through, she announced to J'Nita, as if she had finally decided where to begin: "We'll start in the attic."

Amalya opened the door to the attic and looked up the steep stairs in wonder. J'Nita watched her mother carefully as she patiently waited to follow her to the attic. Amalya thought of the enormous task awaiting them as she began to climb. Slowly her anticipation diminished until she stood near the banister searching with astute scrutiny some familiar things in the cluttered space. In the past, it was sometimes her playroom and Grandma's place for solitude. She studied the years of accumulation; Grandma could never decide what to throw away, but for Amalya, it would make for interesting exploring: What did Grandma like about this? What was that used for? How does that work? Eventually, Amalya would understand what Grandma cherished.

"Be careful not to stumble on anything," she warned J'Nita. The attic reeked of mothballs, cedar and layers of dust. Amalya walked over to a window to open. At first, it was stiff and resistant, having been closed for a duration. Trying to open the window was a physical test of strength and determination. She tried several times but only succeeded in working herself to worried frustration. She and J'Nita looked at the window hopelessly wondering if it would ever open. Perspiration trickled from Amalya's temples as she decided what to do. The attic was without ventilation and they could not remain much longer. Finally, on the last try, the bottom slat separated, letting through a wave of air. Amalya's futility eased only to reassert when she looked around the cluttered room. J'Nita's eyes darted back and forth and then at her mother with understanding and sentiment.

"Grandma kept a lot of things. You wouldn't think all of these things could fit up here."

"Grandma placed things up here all of the time and naturally over the years things accumulated," Amalya explained. Then, she hesitated in thought about the dream. Was it possible that there was such a book in the attic like the one Grandma offered to her? The thought impelled her diligence. She would explore every place in the room until she discovered it. "Where to begin," she questioned as she devised a strategy to find what she believed was among the collection of things.

The breeze from the opened window diluted the stagnant air making it more bearable to be in the attic. Amalya turned to see J'Nita exploring with keen interest some of the items. She didn't interrupt, but decided instead to begin unmasking the clutter single-handedly.

Her hands touched and tossed every kind of item that would be taken from the attic from linens to trowels, metal, wood, plastic, glass, cotton, wool, nylon, boxes, bags. The task of diminishing the clutter started with the first trip and others succeeded. From top to bottom, Amalya trudged the house laden with items to be discarded or put aside for further use. Each time, she was reminded of the innumerable hours Grandma had spent creating a family record. If there was such a record, it had to be in the attic, she surmised. The intrigue possessed her so thoroughly that every item she touched she imagined discovery. So preoccupied was she by the idea, that an ewer fell from her hand and did not come to rest until it landed at the bottom of the stairs with a crash. This startled J'Nita who immediately inquired about the matter.

"It's just this that had fallen," her mother explained as she picked up the ewer and placed it on the counter. J'Nita decided it was time to help her mother

When they returned to the attic, both of them worked assiduously and soon began to see pathways and spaces and the sun brightening the room. Amalya burrowed through every nook and cranny believing she would discover the family record. J'Nita uncovered a pair of rockers and stopped work to try them out. The creaking distracted Amalya and she turned to see J'Nita pushing the chairs forward. She had done the same thing when she first saw them, she smiled. She watched a few moments more and then continued the task. She was more compelled by the idea that there was a family record than ever.

With more of the clutter removed, she finally noticed far back in the corner of the attic, a chest and her hopes ignited. That would be the most likely place to store the family record, she realized. Overwhelmed by the prospect, she decided to go directly to that part of the attic and search through the chest, but was suddenly interrupted by J'Nita.

"Were these yours," J'Nita wanted to know.

"Those rocking chairs," Amalya questioned.

"And the cradle also," J'Nita inquired.

Those rocking chairs are the oldest items in our family. They're hand made so you must be very careful with them. That cradle belonged to every baby who visited Grandma. J'Nita had barely heard her mother's reply as she carefully inspected the items.

The cradle is in perfect condition. The only thing we have to do is dust it and give it a coat of polish. Can we keep it," she pleaded.

"I'm not about to throw it away. Don't you remember Grandma rocking you in that cradle?" Amalya inquired with a smile.

"Me," J'Nita questioned with wonder.

"You and every infant who visited her."

"Then this is an heirloom."

"You can say that," Amalya noted.

J'Nita proceeded to rock it gently and hum in time to its rhythm.

"I thought you remembered Grandma rocking you in that cradle."

"I think I remember now."

"Well, if we intend to make any more progress up here, I think we should continue now."

"How did Grandma find the space," J'Nita wanted to know as she looked around at the many items still left.

"The attic covers the entire house and Grandma saw fit to put everything in it she could not decide to throw away."

"Well, I've found a treasure," commented J'Nita proudly.

"The cradle?" Amalya asked.

"That's right. We're going to keep it, aren't we?"

"We certainly are, but we have to clear away the things round it first. You see, it's just like that chest over there," Amalya direct J'Nita's attention to the far corner of the attic.

"Where," J'Nita questioned as she searched the room until she finally noticed the chest among the disarray. "Yes, I see it now."

"I think that chest contains some valuable items. Sometimes Grandma would spend hours up here alone, and I believe she was working on the family history," explained Amalya.

"You won't be disappointed if she didn't , would you?"

"With all that Grandma left, there's at least one story for every family member."

"I like the cradle," J'Nita noted.

"It does have some interesting stories attached to it that go as far back as I can remember. But first we have to make a path to the chest to find out if there is a record."

Amalya began searching through the items again with the belief that the family record was a grasp away. Moisture formed around her forehead and face as she worked unceasingly to discover what she hoped and believed was in the attic because last evening her grandmother appeared in her dream and, if for no other reason, she believed her grandmother like she always had. She looked intense as if she was racing against time. It's here somewhere, kept searching, she began to prompt her diligence. Soon, what she surmised was confirmed and she didn't have to open the chest to realize it; she only had to remove and open a box to find the family record atop of it. The box was heavy with many items and she thought it best to unpack it rather than move it aside. Amalya was driven like one possessed with a certain imagination; a certain end and a certain ideal that could not be altered until it was fully realized.

When she opened the box, she gasped in surprise from discovery: "Here it is! This is the family record!

J'Nita watched her mother relish in the significance of the discovery. "It's a large book," J'Nita commented as her mother inspected it.

"Yes, but not any book. This book contains stories from at least a century ago; things we could not have dreamed, and what's more important, it's about our ancestors. This record is worth its weight in gold. Why, I believe it dates back to slavery."

"Slavery," J'Nita reiterated with increasing interest as she moved closer to her mother.

"Indeed, if you trace our history, you'll discovery that some of our ancestors were slaves."

"Mama, I'm glad we came to Grandma's today."

"I am too, and now that we found this record, it makes it more special."

"What did Grandma write," J'Nita wanted to know.

"There's a lot here. Grandma spent years gathering what's in this book." Amalya took a cloth and wiped away the dust until it was clear and shiny. She reflected momentarily about what the book might contain: Who were the family members Grandma wrote about? What had taken place during that time? Had she heard Grandma speak any of the names? Then she opened the book and quickly leafed through some of the pages with curious interest to find out.

"What does it say," J'Nita wanted to know.

"There's so much history written here, I can't possibly say it in a few words.

"Can we read some of the pages?"

"I believe Grandma meant for us to read as much as we have to."

"Here," Amalya indicated as she found a place to begin reading. This is what Grandma wrote:" *Daughters and sons: ... The family is like the universe; a world filled with human experiences and promise. We never know what experiences we will have and what promises will be kept, but we do know that family continues the promises.* ... The more Amalya read, the more she cherished what she discovered. She saw names of relatives dating back to slavery she had heard about through conversations from family members, but now she was actually experiencing what she had been told: *I was a slave ... They purchased me from the auction block ... I worked the fields. I don't know my name ... I don't know where I'm from.* As she read, she studied the brown faded ink carefully inscribed on the pages by Grandma and tried to imagine the mysterious world of slavery and what it was like for her ancestors. She could not resist echoing some of the words aloud, as if reiterating them made the reality more impressive. "Grandma recorded what she heard from family members and that is what this book contains," Amalya commented. Here are some other words Grandma wrote from one of our relatives: *Slavery does not make me a lesser person, nor take away my will, I aspired in hulled ships and my spirit remains still.* ... She revered what Grandma had done and held the book as if embracing her spirit in gratitude.

"Grandma was a slave," asked J'Nita.

"No, not Grandma," replied Amalya. "She was born after slavery ended.

Grandma provided a record of our ancestors which includes the great-grands four or five times removed and some of those ancestors were slaves.

J'Nita was both inspired and perplexed about what she heard, but was ignited with interest about the past and did not hesitate to ask: "Can we go back to that time?"

Amalya was astonished and did not know what to reply. Slavery had ended over a century ago and times were different. She really did not know what she thought of that peculiar world that shaped the lives of their ancestors. It was obscure but significant and it was up to her to help J'Nita understand what had taken place. Grandma had found a way, now it was up to her. She began: "We have come a long way since that time; our lives have changed and people are different and the world in which we live is different. She hesitated, noticing that J'Nita still did not comprehend.

"I wish there was a way we could go back to see what it was like during that time," J'Nita pleaded.

Amalya understood her having imagined similar things when she was her age. Not wanting to discourage any hope J'Nita had of understanding the past, she perceived everything had led up to this moment and, if there was anything to hopes and dreams, this was the time to consider what was possible. She looked around at all of the items still left to be sorted and decided one day would not be sufficient, not even two days would suffice. Amalya was inundated with imagination and what was possible; it was the moment when one is driven by extraordinary things that nothing can thwart or stand against. Possibility was infinite. Thus, Amalya proceeded to escort J'Nita over to the rocking chairs and each sat in one of the chairs. There was an uncertain aura about what was about to take place. Amalya still held the family record and remembered the words: "Dreams are wishes," ...and was encouraged. She thought ardently about what she was preparing to do, that is, she and J'Nita were going to travel back to the past. She believed it was possible because the imagination was part of dreams and wishes. She observed J'Nita and saw she was eager to explore beyond. This would far exceed anything she could describe to her about the past and all of those events that was part of their history. She was now more convinced about the idea and announced to J'Nita: "We will dream and imagine and make our wishes until we reach the past.

"How," questioned J'Nita.

Amalya took her hand, without reply, and soon they appeared like they were meditating and nothing could disturb them or break the spell only time and the power of dream and imagination allowed them to soar through time like they were Peter Pan or some other phenomenal sprites. ...

Chapter 3

Searching

Time became light years whirring in boundless space. Amalya and J'Nita could not discern where their imaginations outlasted the uncertainty of what they envisioned could happen. They allowed the gravity of their existence to be thrust to the hilltops and beyond. Moving through time was an effortless journey. Everything was indistinct and vast   Impossibilities soared. Fears transformed. They would not yield to anything that might vanquish them. Sometimes they perceived flashing prisms and saw eclipses of darkness, light obscuring, overshadowing. Then there were indescribable moments. Quiet stillness like they had done nothing; had gone nowhere; had not hoped, dreamed or pursued. They were inanimate, unthinking, unmoving. Time sped in light years. Histories coiled into other histories until finally there was no disguising, no repelling only observing. Was this the time, they wondered; was this the place, they yearned; were people there or about, they searched: Aware, unaware, converging, mindful of necessities they could not remit. Eyes beholding: Humans tied to others; constricted, bound - inextricably bound. Their apprehension confounded like the mysteries they encountered and drove them to the edge of despair. Repressing the outcry of reboant sounds of those being auctioned; quickly sold and indifferently carried away to be separated for life, Amalya and J'nita recognized they were experiencing the place and time in history of their ancestors. They were in the mysterious past Grandma wrote about. They could see their ancestors, but they could not be seen; they could touch them, but they could not be felt; it was like they were invisible and in a dream-like awareness....

. The silence of the night pervaded the land. Cabins etched across the sprawling and palatial acreage. Amalya and J'Nita would not see the natural beauty of the grounds and rolling hills until daybreak. Then the tall trees would overwhelm them, the lush grass, the rivers and lakes and fertile land would captivate them and make them awed. They believed they had settled where their ancestors began according to family history and according to what Grandma had written. The Thornton's were the ancestors who began their family in Georgia. Their kinship extended far and wide and sustained through the peculiar conditions of the plantation. The dichotomies of what existed and wielded upon the lives of their ancestors were apparent. Their ancestors had lived life solitarily through the plantation. Their ancestors had suffered; had grown and had outlasted the cruel fate of slavery, of servitude, of lashes and of toil. When Amalya and J'Nita witnessed what life was like for their ancestors, they were reminded: "life was not easy; it was one continuous strain of toil and adversity."

Thus, they were endeared when they finally saw what they believed was the first Thornton family. Their eyes connected not bodily but by spirit and knowledge of what they had always heard and imagined about the life of their ancestors. They were inundated with thought and emotions the longer the images of the Thornton family remained.

They first saw Mama Thornton who sat upright summoning her children in a resolute voice. She seemed undaunted by the circumstances as she awaited her children's response. One by one each of them appeared. Jacque, who was the oldest, was tall, with broad shoulders and moved with quick impatience, followed by Samuel and Elijah who were light in statute, and possessed a keen agility of mind. They doted on their mother's concerns and were always eager to know her intentions. All of them solemnly waited for the daughters to appear.

As if it would speed the appearance of their sisters, Jacque and Elijah would stand instead of sitting on the wooden, straight backed chairs in the room. They stared hypnotically at their looming shadows cast in the dim room by two burning lanterns on opposite tables. They silently ruminated about the many nights they had gone to the edge of the river hoping to escape. They yearned for freedom more than life, but when they thought of their mother, they repelled. They scrutinized their mother who was quiet with reserve. They had such reverence for her that they would not as much as impose one question in favor of their acute curiosity to reveal her purpose. Instead, they deferred and remained patient.

Soon their sisters, Emily and Leona appeared. They were younger but seemingly mature. Jacque immediately voiced mild admonition to them about keeping their mother waiting. They stared apologetically and sat next to their mother. Jacque did not feel he would be out of order if he informed their mother that all were present. His manner was forceful and he spoke with a firm voice: "Mama, all of us are here now." They felt liberated and eager to hear their mother's intentions, but she remained vigilant and searched the room as if expecting other children to arrive. Scrutinizing the children before her, she regarded their maturity with adulation. She relished that they were still together, but cautioned that, without warning, any one of them could be taken away.

After moments of contemplation, Mama Thornton informed them: "All of you are not here.

Knowing that their mother could sometimes overlook things, Samuel spoke in their defense: "Yes, we're all here. I'm Samuel, there's Jacque, Elijah, Emily and Leona."

"No, all of you are not here," she insisted.

A stir of confusion ensued among them as Mama Thornton plunged into brooding about the children who had disappeared.

Amalya and J'Nita felt on the verge of distress feeling that something had gone wrong. Their emotions plunged. Their compassion swelled. What had happened? Who was not there? One question succeeded another, as they waited to hear. ...

Each day Mama Thornton watched her children go into the fields, and each time she was not certain if they would return until they reappeared at the end of day. One day held the agonizing memory that she likens to the death of her husband. She could not do anything about death, but escape of her children, she always wondered if she could have prevented the misfortune. Many times, she had heard about slaves who had escaped to freedom, but it never occurred to her in her most profound imaginings that some of her children were plotting their escape. When it was certain they had run away, it arrested her like death. Every place they had been, she expected them to appear as they usually had: in the fields, through the doors of the cabin, in the rooms. She could not believe they had eloped to an unknown place. Their images were like illusions that gave her hope and then were gone in a glance; that's what her missing children had become to her – specters in the night that appeared and disappeared almost simultaneously. In time, she had to resign to the fact that she would never see them again.

The absence of the siblings did not go unquestioned by the younger children who immediately wanted to know where they were. Mama Thornton put forth many defenses until they were deterred from asking any more questions about them. When she could face up to the fact that her children were missing, she gathered them together one day and gave a terse explanation: "The older children have gone away," she said in acknowledgement of the children's mysterious disappearance. Her children stared at her painfully hoping she would explain more, but she did not. Thus, they were left to wonder if their siblings were sold to another plantation or had run away.

In time, the children learned that their siblings had run for freedom. To them it sounded incredible, but what their siblings had done had become lore: They had run for freedom and they believed they were free citizens somewhere. "Freedom's every man's dream," Jacque would comment proudly. Once he learned what happened, he realized it wasn't about forgiveness or being forsaken or anything like that, but about the rights of every slave to be free. "One day, one day, freedom for me," he would remind them wistfully.

Mama Thornton was not as accepting of her children's actions and could not condone their deeds for any cause. She knew she had to give account to Master Thornton and convince him that she did not know where they were or had anything to do with their disappearance. At that moment she seemed to be reliving the agony of confronting Master Thornton when her children disappeared. ...

The servants at Master Thornton's house watched her intently, wondering what would be done about her children. Everyone knew about the incident. It was talked about and surmised by everyone. Many wondered if Mama Thornton conspired for many knew the desire for freedom was great and her children had not returned after many weeks. Mama Thornton's anxiety deepened as curious eyes looked accusingly at her. They were condemning her whether she had something to do with or children's escape or not. The children were still missing.

Amalya and J'Nita had not anticipated what they were witnessing. Their ancestors were being accused of actions that had dire consequences and Mama Thornton especially was liable for punishment. Their first reaction was to help, but they couldn't and that distressed them further. They could only wonder what the master would do to Mama Thornton. ...

Master Thornton deliberately stalled for time. He knew that if Mama Thornton were guilty of any untoward thing that her conscience would be telling. He had known fugitives to profess their guilt once captured. Then too, he knew that Mama Thornton and her family had been on the plantation before he was born and were in good standing. There had never been any incident, but this was a different time and an urgent matter. He was in a dilemma what to do. He knew Mama Thornton fairly well, but he also knew that freedom compelled slaves more than anything.

Mama Thornton was so overwhelmed with anxiety that whatever she thought to tell Master Thornton about the incident was forgotten and only a dark void like blindness loomed. If only her children knew what conflict it caused her and if only they knew she prayed for their lives wherever they were; she hoped they were alive and well. The dire thought of never seeing them again arrested her as it had the day she resigned to the fact that they had escaped. When Master Thornton spoke every thought was numb, not a word flowed from her mind.

"You know why I have called you here," he began.

Mama Thornton barely nodded an understanding as she contended with the turmoil within her. Sometimes she heard Master Thornton and sometimes she saw him as a child she had once nurtured, but time had made the past a thing of memory. He was determined to pursue his inquiry.

"Your children have fled the plantation and are now fugitives. It's an unfortunate thing to happen; they could be killed if they are caught. I have no control over what the patrollers might do to them."

As Master Thornton spoke, "Mama's alarm increased. The word _killed_ made her realize what grave danger her children faced – the ultimate consequences awaited them. She had heard of such things and had imagined what it was like, but never did she think any of her children would be in such a predicament.

"Do you know anything about what happened," asked Master Thornton somberly. She had awaited that question and didn't know what to answer then and was still at a loss for words. But she gathered her composure because she was their mother and had to explain something. She couldn't say she didn't know anything because she was their mother, she had to know something, thus she began to explain.

"Every morning I call my children and they appear. I called and called my children that morning and some of them appeared and others didn't. I warned them to appear immediately or else. When I say that they know what will happen, but still they did not appear. Finally, the other children say, "they not there, they're gone." "Gone, I asked, where?" They say they didn't know. Well, to my disappointment, they never came out of the room. They had disappeared. I didn't know what I would do. I thought maybe they would appear that evening, but they didn't. I waited many days hoping they would. I was fearful because I realized something was wrong."

She grew silent as Master Thornton considered her explanation. His dilemma was the insurgence came from a family that never caused any trouble. Mama Thornton had been on the plantation all of her life. The longer he studied Mama Thornton, the more convinced he became that she had no part in her children's actions. After considerable thought, he decided: "I will not hold you liable for what your children did. I will, however, hold you liable for what your other children might do. His decision made her feel exonerated for she had imagined the harshest punishment. She was relieved when Master Thornton accepted her explanation as truth. But he did not tell her she could leave and she was waiting for that and wondering why she was still there.

Master Thornton arose from his chair and walked over to the window, peering through. His manner had changed. What was the matter, thought Mama Thornton. Now, she felt nearly the same troubling emotions she had when she arrived. She had to look towards him; to see the sun, the shadow and the man-child peering through the window like staring at life. Maybe, he knew about her children. Fear arose in her like never before and it had to do with something far greater than anything she could imagine.

Something had occurred. The future was beckoning, and she listened.

"I have traveled around this region and there's a changing tide growing in our midst. I'm not sure when it will rise up and destroy everything around us, but there's talk about emancipation."

"Emancipation," inquired Mama Thornton incomprehensively.

"The slaves will become free." He added

To Mama Thornton what he said sounded incredible. Never did she think she would hear such a theory from Master Thornton under any circumstances. She now wondered if she heard correctly.

"Master," she interrupted.

"Now, now, there's no need to worry just yet. In fact, before anything happens, I would like to put forth a proposition. I've already mentioned that you will be responsible for the actions of your other children. You need not despair about it for I propose if anything should happen to you at any time, your children will be free."

"Free," Mama Thornton reiterated in astonishment. "My children will be free." The words resounded in her mind over and over. The prospect was like a long awaited dream. All of the generations she knew, including hers had lived without freedom, but now her children might be manumitted, and their children children's children – in perpetuity. It was unreal, she thought as she pursued the possibilities. The image of her children in freedom was prodigious.

"I don't know what to say. It sounds like a promise of a dream," she commented.

"Propositions have conditions, Master Thornton reminded her. You and your children must understand what those are," he cautioned. He then detailed to

Mama his proposal, but nothing as important as the word *freedom* held a greater impact. Mama Thornton ascended the realm of freedom for several moments; it was the closest she had ever come to being free when she imagined her children in freedom. If Master Thornton had not demanded her verbal understanding about the proposition, she would not have considered it possible, but she gave him her earnest assurance that she understood. Freedom is the only thing for all people, she thought as she walked out of the room euphoric and regretful that her other children would never realize how fate could have transformed their lives also.

It had been years since the meeting with Master Thornton and much had transpired; mainly, her children were now young men and women with impatience and disagreeable temperaments and now this was another occasion she had to remind them; "All of you are not here," she repeated. They looked at her and then at each other for they knew what would follow.

"Mama, you talking about those siblings that runaway to freedom," asked Jacque to make certain.

"I don't know if they found freedom or not, I haven't heard a word about them in all these years. Naturally, I been wondering since they run off without warning."

Jacque, Elijah and Samuel looked t each other furtively and with a sense of guilt because they never told their mother what they learned about the other siblings.

You can't hold it against them for looking for freedom," commented Elijah.

"All over this land there are uprisings from slaves looking for freedom. There are people speaking out against it. In Harper's Ferry, the great mountains trembled, there were protesters mounting against slavery, battles are about to be waged."

"Jacque," shouted Mama Thornton frightfully, remembering what Master Thornton had explained to her, "we're all in the same boat and we shouldn't turn it over because we might perish. Henry, Mandolin and Ezekiel have done enough. We don't know if they drowned or reached shore."

"There are places in this land where there's freedom for us," Jacque added.

"That might be true, but don't go running off like them, you might not find it. Let freedom come to you. I haven't heard a word from them in all these years, not one word," Mama complained sadly.

Whenever Mama Thornton reminded them of that sad fact, her children were at a lost to console her; they knew how deeply affected she was about the older sibling's disappearance.

"The patrollers got the, that's what happened," Leona exclaimed.

"You're too young to understand, that's why you say such things," Emily chided.

"I've heard about patrollers," Leona retorted.

"We heard about the patrollers too, but that don't mean they caught our siblings," Emily reasoned as she noticed the way Jacque glared with approbation about what the other siblings had done. She wanted to caution him in case their mother became suspicious of him. All of the siblings knew that Jacque wanted to escape and talked about it often, and they were fearful that any day they would awaken and he would be gone like the other siblings who escaped to freedom.

"Just think, Mama, our siblings are free citizens somewhere in this land and that's a proud thing," Jacque lauded.

"They don't want to look back now if they free," Elijah added.

"We're slaves," said Emily reminding them of their predicament.

"I'm not a slave," Leona said defensively.

"You're a slave whether you like it or not," Jacque reminded her.

With guarded frustration, Leona turned to Mama and asked: "Am I a slave?"

Mama was careful not to take sides or create any conflict among them, thus she replied; "Daughter, you're my last and youngest child." The other siblings were outwitted as Leona seemed appeased.

"You hear Mama, I'm not a slave. You see, one day things are going to be different. I'll walk this countryside and feel what freedom is. It won't be nothing to stop me, no lashes, no river, I'll cross the river and go to the great camp ground 'cause I'll be free."

"Mama!" Jacque interrupted in agitation, "Leona is thinking uppity."

"Don't mind those things, Leona, it's not good to get your hopes up."

Leona gave a downcast stare and became silent.

"She's always talking about dreams and freedom. I tell her she's too young to understand," commented Emily.

"Leona is beside herself," complained Jacque.

"Don't think beside yourself," Mama admonished Leona.

"Yes, Mama," said Leona.

"One day freedom will come for all of us," Mama reminded them.

Mama re-ignited the interest of Elijah, John and Samuel who stared pensively hoping Mama would explain more for presently they were beyond the realm of the plantation and thinking about freedom.

"There are those people, …what they called," Elijah wondered.

"Abolitionist," Samuel reminded him anxiously.

"That's right, abolitionists," Elijah repeated. "They are the people who want to end slavery."

Fear arose in Mama again upon hearing what her children were openly expressing. She labored to suppress her apprehensions about what they were alluding to. When she could no longer tolerate her trepidations, she voiced her concerns to them.

"We have to be careful talking about such things because the abolitionists don't live on this plantation. Word get around that the Thornton's stirring up trouble, you know what will happen."

"Elijah knew that Mama's admonishment was intended to keep peace among them, thus he acceded: We'll be careful."

"There are people working to end slavery. Freedom's spreading around this land. There are more people escaping to freedom than ever before," Samuel noted.

"That might be true," Mama acknowledged, "but nobody hears word."

"Yes, there's word," Jacque divulged.

"About my children," Mama questioned with keen interest.

"No," he replied, "we haven't heard nothing about our siblings, but we have heard tell of slaves reaching freedom."

"Whether the other children reached freedom or not, there's not a day that I don't wonder what happened to them. That's what I'm thinking now," Mama admitted with dejection.

"We don't know, Mama," said Jacque.

"We sad to say, we can't tell you about our siblings," added Elijah.

The proposition that was offered by Master Thornton many years ago had become nothing more than a broken promise to Jacque and the other siblings. Too many years had passed for them to believe it would ever happen, but Mama wanted them to maintain hope anyway and she reminded them often.

"I'm not one for inspiring the wrong expectations, but freedom is going to come to you one day and it's sooner than you believe. When it does, remember what I've told you and remember your other siblings who run away. I believe they out there in the land like fallen branches waiting to be picked up and looked after. Don't forget children, I dream of the day all of you will meet and come together – free."

Encouraged again by what her mother explained, Emily promised: When we free, I won't stop searching for our siblings until hope runs its course.

"That's the spirit, my child," said Mama with optimism. "I might not see freedom, but I pray for my children. Lord, I do wonder about freedom. Jacque, she called.

Jacque, along with his brothers, had been listening and realized more than ever what a thin line it was between the river and freedom. They only had to reach the river and cross it. That's what their siblings did and the other slaves who escaped to freedom.

"Jacque," Mama called again.

"Yes, Mama," he finally responded.

"You lead," she requested.

"You want us to sing that song you like," he asked to make certain.

"Jacque turned to the others and prepared them to join him in singing: "Swing Low, Sweet Chariot." Jacque's voice was a deep baritone that commanded the lyrics and gave them life. Leona's high, soprano voice was like a shrill waving through the low tones to bring harmony to the song and motion of the chariot moving.

When Amalya and J'Nita heard them sing, it reminded them of Grandma and for a brief moment they relieved the day of Grandma's home going, but they were not sad this time, but understood why Grandma loved the song.

Mama Thornton seemed to drift into another world; her mind was at ease. When her children noticed her resting, they went to the other room and continued to sing and talk.

"Freedom will be a day to see," John remarked wistfully.

"It won't be long, I been telling you," Leona commented.

"Little Sis, you sleep and wake and wake and sleep, but freedom is found clear across the land and sometimes you can't sleep at all to find your way.

"I know we'll be free soon," Leona insisted.

"Your kind of freedom is tied to dreams and imagination. You're entitled to your dreams, why dreams are as ancient as the world and we can't stop them, but freedom, we got to run for it." Jacque had driven the demons of fear away as he spoke about freedom. Many times he and his brothers had been on the verge of escaping when they heard about more slaves reaching freedom. The prospect of freedom always held its power and was unresolved in his mind.

His sisters noticed the confidence Jacque had when he talked about freedom and were fearful, not so much about his boasting, but thinking how they would be left alone and how they would manage, along with Mama. The older they got, they realized, it was just a matter of time that he and his other brothers would escape, but that did not stop them from prompting them otherwise.

"Mama said let freedom find us here on this plantation."

"Yes," Emily sided quickly. "You know you been getting ideas about running away, but we promised Mama we would be here until that time. You know that's the proposition we would be free."

"That's been some years ago," Jacque commented impatiently. "No telling about that now."

"Just the same, you can't run off from here," Emily insisted.

"What give you suspicion," Jacque wanted to know.

Emily confronted him directly and stared him down testing his mettle. "Jacque you have, haven't you?"

"Why truth is, if I didn't think about freedom, I wouldn't be a man. A man has to see the sun and steamboats rolling up the river to other lands."

"Jacque," Emily prompted, "I don't think Mama means for her remaining children to insurrect. Why you think she called us here?"

The mere mention of the word *freedom* inspired Jacque as he responded: "I don't know Little Sis, but I believe Mama explained her account and made us promise to look up our siblings when we reach freedom." Jacque then reminded his siblings of all the gallant slaves fighting for freedom and he, too, would be like the abolitionists and help others to freedom.

"Great deeds will always be remembered by courageous people who help others. I wonder if our siblings found the Underground Railroad before they reached freedom," questioned Emily.

Hearing *Underground Railroad* from Emily sounded an alarm in Jacque. "You know about the Underground Railroad?" he wanted to know.

"Certainly, I know about the Underground Railroad," replied Emily proudly.

"You planning to use it one day," questioned Jacque.

"You mean like you, Elijah and Samuel?"

Jacque turned away in denial as Emily leered with absolute knowledge.

"We ain't for sure," Elijah finally conceded.

"No, we ain't for sure," Samuel admitted.

"You see," said Emily, if only Mama knew.

Leona seized the moment to voice her indignation: "Jacque, Elijah and Samuel, you mean to tell me y'all been planning to escape like the others. I can't believe what I'm hearing. Freedom is almost here, and if you let it come to you like Mama say, you won't have to look over your shoulders to see who might be coming for you."

"We made a promise to Mama," reminded Emily. "She's getting up in years; it might be any year or day, but a promise is a promise."

"I know what a promise is," said Jacque with a charged attitude. Why promises and dreams are all we be living on."

"That's hope, Jacque, and we got to have that," Emily commented.

"Master told Mama years ago we be free if something happens to her and that was a long time ago," Jacque reflected somberly.

"In other words, we won't be liable for slavery any more. That's something to think about. One way or the other, freedom isn't far from us," explained Emily.

"Our other siblings didn't look back. The Underground Railroad provided the way for them and they didn't have to worry about nothing but the chance. They escaped free and clear," Jacque brooded and was not able to relinquish the prospects of freedom.

"It's a risk," Emily cautioned. "We don't know if our other siblings are free or slave and even worse, whether they are dead or alive. We haven't heard a word and that's disturbing. You want that burden knowing what it will do to Mama."

Sometimes it was hard for Jacque and his brothers to weigh a decision about whether to escape to freedom. Each day became more difficult for them to endure. They thought if they could reach freedom, they might be able to free the other Thornton's. That was their compelling dream. Again, they were confronted with their intentions about the proposition Mama assured them was made by Master Thornton. Jacque turned to Elijah and Samuel and for a long time they stared and contemplated until finally they reasserted their understanding: "A promise is a promise," Jacque mumbled.

"We got to stand up to that," Elijah agreed.

"I guess there's no getting around it," Samuel added.

"Master say we will be free if anything happens to Mama," Jacque asked for reassurance.

"That's right," Emily replied with certainty. "In other words, we won't be liable for slavery no more. We'll be free and so will our children, and their children. "It's something to think about. You must believe that, Jacque."

"It's settled now Little Sis; Mama won't have to worry because we give our word," Jacque commented finally. "Now that Mama be resting, you think we can hum a little of "Steal Away.""

"Jacque, I declare, freedom driving you away," exclaimed Emily.

"It's a song, Little Sis, just a song. I'm a man of my words."

The subject of escape once again drifted into the unsettled wills of the Thornton's as they prepared to sing a few hymns as was their habit to lull the night. No cares were considered, just peace and tranquility like slavery never existed.

Amalya and J'Nita listened to their ancestors sing until their voices faded and the night closed; no sounds were heard, not even a flutter of a butterfly.

Chapter 4

Free Alas!

Amalya and J'Nita were lulled into a kind of oblivion and did not know when the illuminations of the past had ceased. They only perceived that the previous awareness had disappeared and their ancestors were not visible. The darkness surrounded them like an insurmountable void. The void remained unseeing and unhearing for so long, Amalya and J'Nita wondered if they had seen all of their ancestors and the past, but were careful not to make a sudden outcry that would revert them.

They could not see or feel time revolving, but the years rolled through a span of more than a decade. Change strung a long thread of possibilities, unimagined and coveted. The people were different, the plantation and society had changed like an unknown cause had appeared and destroyed everything that once existed. Emancipation flourished in the hearts and minds of the people and society like never before. Amalya and J'Nita tried to comprehend what they envisioned for it was far different than they expected. They had to look far and wide to recognize their ancestors.

When the darkness lifted, the status of the Thornton's was remarkably transformed. Amalya and J'Nita had followed the mobility of Emily and Leona for a sustained period before they realized who they were. It was like nature had made them different people - not so much in years as in physical difference. They were uncertain of who they were until they heard one of them utter "Jacque!" and it was then they knew where they were.

Emily and Leona had outgrown their puberty and were mature young women in search of understanding and acceptance of what had taken place. They had barely gotten through their puberty when, suddenly, like an act of God, their lives were thrust into a new light. Presently, they were still ordering and comprehending the details about the demise of the previous Thornton life. They did not take the newly acquired status for granted; sometimes they were so skeptical, they suspected any day their freedom would be rescinded. It took time and time alone for Emily and Leona not to be haunted by their inner suspicions. Sometimes they were so intense and inwardly pensive about their trepidations, their bright eyes and caramel complexion appeared dim. When they could no longer tolerate their apprehensions individually and solely, they would indulge in conversation about the circumstances leading up to and following the milestone that finally willed freedom for the Thornton men and women. They could now hold their heads high but skepticism made them humble; they could go far beyond the plantation, but fear made them repel.

There was more joy than they ever knew existed, but there was sadness also. Every morning they were reminded about the memories and emotions indelibly etched in their minds about what had occurred.

"Mama was as close to freedom as you can get," Leona began. "Her last words keep me thinking how close she was to freedom."

"It's not like she's gone, her soul is soaring now," Emily reminded.

"I know, I know, I always feel Mama's here right now, but it's different you know like blind faith, you feel the truth of it."

"We glad we free, but we sad because Mama's not here; she is the reason we free, we'll never forget that and she wouldn't want us to."

"No, no, she wouldn't because we kept our promise; I don't think we would be the same if we hadn't," Leona reminded.

Silence interrupted them as if they expected their mother to appear or to call them as she was accustomed to doing, but when it didn't happen, Leona continued: "You remember Jacque?"

"You mean Jacque, Samuel and Elijah," Emily added. "I sure do; they were so overcome, all they could say was 'Mama, we made our promise and we keep our word." It'll be a long time before we forget'." That was all Mama needed to hear. It was like those words made her free because she was gone afterwards. There was an eerie silence and this place was never the same," Emily commented sadly.

"That's to be expected," consoled Leona. Remember, Mama said you can slave the body, but not the soul; the soul is forever free."

"We were never as happy as when Master handed us those papers making us free," Emily recounted with enlightened memory.

"I always knew we would live to see freedom," commented Leona with revelation. Master said: 'The children of Viola Littlejohn a/k/a Viola Thornton, are now free! If you mean to leave the plantation, you'll need to take these papers with you. It won't be long all slaves will be free.'"

"I declare, I didn't know what to do or what to think," exclaimed Emily. Everything changed in an instant!"

"I was lost for words," admitted Leona. "Did you see the change in Jacque when he took those papers making him a free man. He examined them and turned them over and over like they were gold. I think those papers meant more to him than anything else in this world. I watched him and I could just see him traveling away from here in a hurry because he was a free man."

"Indeed, indeed. It must have been an overwhelming burden for him to stay as he promised Mama, but he was one for his word."

"It took months for him to gather himself. I thought he was deciding to stay; I was hoping he would stay," revealed Leona.

"It took that long because of his wife and child," Emily explained. "He couldn't leave them regardless to the circumstances and not knowing if he would ever return again. That bothered me, but I couldn't hold it against him because he made certain about Mama."

"He visited her grave every day until at some point, it was like Mama finally bid him farewell. He summoned us around her grave and made his peace, and caused us to make our peace also. All of us gathered and sang: "I Done What Ya' Told Me To Do."

So glad I done, so glad I done, so glad I done
What ya' told me to do.
So glad I done, so glad I done, so glad I done
What ya' told me to do
Told me to pray and I prayed
So glad I done, so glad I done, so glad I done
What ya' told me to do
Thank God I done what ya' told me to do
So glad I done, so glad I done, so glad I done
What ya' told me to do.

They sang and hummed the verses again inspired about the day death made their flight to freedom precarious.

"Jacque said: 'Sorry Mama couldn't see me leave a free man. I'm going north; I'm free and free is how I will remain.' Goodness, he was afraid his freedom wasn't real. We were uncertain also. We had to keep looking at those papers to know it was real."

"Yes, I remember," Leona agreed. "We wished him well and a safe journey. The creaking wheels of Papa's wagon started stiff and resistant, but it became a smoother ride as Jacque and his family rode away from the plantation headed north. I never imagined the wagon would be used by Jacque and his family to leave the plantation. I was thinking: "Don't break down now; the north star will be your guide. I watched until the only thing I could see was dust and shadows on the horizon.""

"Elijah and Samuel wanted to go, but said they would journey later. Their minds were on courtship and lucky for us because that would have been a lot of absence to tolerate," Emily admitted.

"Jacque was following his dreams. It gave us a new light too, but what were we to do with it?" Leona was still wondering.

"Don't dwell on it. We free to leave any time we want; that's when you know you're free. You hear Master say it won't be long before all slaves be free," reminded Emily.

"It's our hope," said Leona wistfully. …

The day slavery ceased to be was a long time coming even before the Thornton's yearned, there had been other families, men women and children who had the will and determination to be free, but those virtues were not the only endowments needed to make a person free. It took an entire country, conflict, debate and civil war. Amalya and J'Nita realized it was why Jacque and the other children were so cautious. Their decision to stay the course of promise was compounded with skepticism. They weighed the odds their siblings faced and concluded it was nearly impossible. The day they were free ended much of their consternation about why they had became hopeless. Amalya and J'Nita exulted in their ancestor's endurance and wanted to break through the illusion and embrace them, but had to remain and watch their ancestors disappear.

Dark forms spread across the expanse; nothing moved, spoke, complained, gave voice or command. Amalya and J'Nita could not determine whether people lived or died, or whether there was a world. Everything was silent and still like life had ceased. Nothingness became the order and power. Amalya and J'Nita were fearful and wondered if they had gotten stranded or halted in time. Again, they began to doubt what they pursued until they heard a creaking, familiar sound. They listened and watched closely until the void lifted and a pristine and vast land appeared. They noticed an object approaching from a distance and the creaking sound became louder and louder. They weren't sure what it was until it neared. When the obscurity cleared, they noticed without a doubt it was Jacque and his family headed north. ...

Jacque clutched the reins and stared straight ahead at the horizon. The fact that he was free had a daunting effect; he was still uncertain about his destiny. It was a strange mystery he was trying to understand. From the day he knew he was a slave, he yearned for freedom. Now he was free, he felt a different burden: he could not obliterate the past immediately. Neither the miles nor the rest of the years he had to live could obliterate his former life, he realized. As he rode across the strange land, diverse emotions disturbed his illusions of freedom, the greatest emotions being those of fear and doubt. The land was desolate and vast and he felt dwarfed for a sustained period as he drove. He noticed the clouds passing and the sun glaring and other times he only noticed what was within him which enabled him to continue his journey north.

His wife, Willa was sometimes aware and other times completely absorbed in the care of their infant. She was an attractive, medium sized woman with scarf draped around her head and shoulders, long enough to wrap and secure the infant.

From time to time Jacque would check on them to make certain of their safety especially when the infant fretted. Usually, Willa was able to calm the infant immediately. Seeing that both Willa and the infant were solaced, Jacque was apt to voice some of his thoughts to Willa.

"A man can't be too careful along this road. We have to ride as far away as possible from danger; don't want no trouble while we're riding north."

"Those papers Master give you says you're a free man," Willa reminded him.

"That what's written on these papers," he said as he touched the place where he put them to make certain they were still there. "I'm a free man. I declare, I had great hope but I didn't dream that I would ever live to see the day. Take a long look as we journey to freedom, there will be memories in every trail of dust. Those memories are our history; that's what slavery is and now, that's what freedom is – our history.

"Time will take care of it; it's just starting," Willa consoled.

"I think time made us partners as indelible as the sun," commented Jacque. "Some days those memories search us and remind us who we are."

"We don't have to worry no more about working in the sun," Willa reminded him. "We're free, the baby is free too. She won't worry like we do."

Jacque stared at his daughter resting against Willa; she *is* free, he realized. She will not have to endure the barriers they did. She can face life and not have to wait for freedom or pray for freedom like they did. He felt a qualm stir within him. His fears about slavery had not vanished. He would have to reach north and live in freedom to know the true meaning. Jacque was reminded of other things also when he looked at his child.

"Our daughter carries Mama's name. Each day I see her, I will think of Mama and never forget the promise of freedom that came through her. Our daughter will be one of the multitudes who will sing: "Many Thousands Gone"

No more peck o'corn for me, no more, nor more,
No more driver's lash for me
No more pint o'salt for me
No more hundred lash for me
No more mistress' call for me
No more no more, many thousand gone. ...

"That's what it's going to be like for our children," said Jacque as he caressed the infant.

"We leaving slavery, no more looking back," Willa managed to comment.

Jacque became sullen as he was reminded what his life was like on the plantation. "I waited the day I would be like a bird soaring in the sky; that's freedom to me."

"They say freedom is going to come to every slave; it's just a matter of time it be written into law," commented Willa.

"That's what I hear, but the Master give me these papers and that's freedom to me now. If it becomes law of the land, I still have these papers to show I'm free. Freedom is when you can feel it just like we're beginning," Jacque explained.

"Is that why you left the plantation," Willa wanted to know. Jacque considered a reply and thought about all of the times he wanted to escape and the dream he had of being free. There were many reason, some more apparent than others. Even though he was free, he could not readily perceive the difference.

"Maybe it has to do with a lot of things, I can't put into words," he finally replied.

"There might come a time south is going to be like north and when we travel south, we going to say south looks like north. That's what change can do. Do you think that day will be," Willa questioned.

"You mean that I go back to Georgia," Jacque asked. He knew that everyone had expected him to leave the plantation once he became free, but they never thought he would actually leave. They thought once he became free, he would reconsider and remain on the plantation like his brothers and sisters.

"The horizon I see has north written on it and is far from the plantation," Jacque replied.

When Jacque first told Willa that they were leaving the plantation, she thought he was talking about a dream. He was always talking about the north and freedom and how one day they would leave the plantation as free citizens. She thought those were impossible dreams, but he was entitled to talk about them anyway. She liked the sound of freedom and the way Jacque described it. Sometimes she became afraid to hear him talk about such things as freedom knowing what happened to his siblings, but when he showed her the papers one day, she started to believe him. Day after day the questions posed: Was it real? Was it true? Would they actually leave the plantation? It was all she could do not to question the reality of what she saw. It was not until Jacque assembled the wagon, that the dawn of a new life began; they were destined to journey north and experience freedom as he had dreamed.

"Suddenly, they were interrupted by the child's crying again. Jacque watched her writhe uncomfortably as Willa tried to console her.

"We stopping along the road," she asked as she lulled the infant.

"I made some allowances; soon as we cross the Georgia border," Jacque informed her.

"You found a road without patrollers," Willa observed.

"Patrollers haven't been this way yet. No need to worry about them, I got my papers to show I'm a free man."

The infant began to cry again causing both of them to be concerned.

"I don't know what's the matter with her," Willa complained as she tried to quiet the infant.

"She ain't never rode to freedom," commented Jacque. "Little daughter, no need crying now, we free. Crying ain't for freedom." The infant gradually quieted and remained calm as they traveled many more miles.

The expansive world before him increased his anticipation. He wondered, with enlightened prospect what the north would be like. He could clearly see the new land he was pursuing for it was where he was destined. The touch of the reins was like the pulling strength of his determination, hope and reason for living. The word free insinuated from the very depths of his being; the impossible was becoming his life – free forever.

When Jacques estimated that they were beyond Georgia, they stopped and rested. He anchored the wagon nearby and built a camp, spreading blankets and bundles to rest upon. Both Jacque and Willa were bewildered about the vast world surrounding them and stared for what seemed an eternity believing it would disappear, and when it did not, Jacque moved unsteadily around the space inspecting it with curious wonder. It was harvest and everything seemed to move frantically gathering. It reminded him of the plantation; it was that season that gave him hope; hope of a promise and things to come. It was hard for him to leave the plantation during this time, but he believed he would reap another promise. He thought of his mother and siblings and was not diminished about his decision to journey north because he realized that one day there will be another harvest. He ventured beyond; recollecting the opportunities he heard that existed in the north. For the first time, he did not repel hopelessly but pursued the possibilities of his dreams. Each thought became like the light weight of a cloud moving effortlessly in the sky; the illumination of freedom was vast, nothing was excluded as he ventured further until the day yielded a darkening sky. During that time, Jacque had expended every possibility of his dreams. It was hard to undo what was entrenched within him all of those years at the plantation: the repressive, fettered existence was overwhelming, but in spite of his burdens, he perceived greater depths of freedom than he ever thought possible. He was a destined man, destined to expand all possibilities of his newly acquired freedom. He was now anxious to rest so that he could continue the journey north.

"All night I will be staring at the sky," he thought aloud. "Sky plays host to dreams. It's intended we reach north; it's written up there in destiny. It is my hope that one day there will be no color boundary or slavery."

Jacque watched the sky change from pale gray to dark blue with stars glimmering and shining. The glares of light were hypnotic causing him drowsiness. He looked at Willa and the infant who were already resting, and eventually he slept also.

Since the beginning of the journey, Jacque had repressed the fear that they could possibly encounter patrollers. He knew that the patrollers had the authority to return them to the plantation, sell them or even kill them. The thought was so terrifying, he had placed a barrier enormous enough to bar intrusion. But, in the scrim between the conscious and unconscious what was deeply embedded became apparent. It was a terrible nightmare when he saw visions of patrollers pursuing him, drawing closer and closer, stopping and hovering over him. He tried desperately to rid the images, but he was too weary and the fear too great; he could not disengage. Now he was listening. At first they were barely audible words, indistinct and meaningless utters. Gradually, however, Jacque began to comprehend when he heard the word *plantation*. Thoughts enlightened that reminded him he was a free man and had papers to prove what had occurred. Soon, he became poised and confident as his fears were presently allayed.

The presence of the men loomed. Jacque could see them visibly and clearly.

"What plantation you from," the men wanted to know.

"We are resting a while," Jacque replied.

"This ain't no place for you to be resting, this is wilderness," explained the patrollers.

"I'm a free man," Jacque informed them proudly.

"Free," the patrollers questioned derisively. "Ain't no free slaves here. You must be one of those abolitionists," they surmised suspiciously.

"No sir, I'm not an abolitionists, I'm a freeman and have papers to prove it," Jacque explained as he reached for the papers. He searched and searched, but discovered they were missing. He momentarily plunged into panic and despair as he tried to remember where he put the papers. He sensed a mockery unfolding and he also sensed the growing impatience of the patrollers.

"Sir," Jacque began in a somber voice, "we're weary from traveling. Master give us permission to leave the plantation."

"Where are the papers," the patrollers insisted eager to see them.

Jacque could not explain the disappearance of the papers and the predicament he now faced. He was certain of what happened that caused him to be on the journey north. He recalled vividly the day master said: "The children of Viola Littlejohn aka Viola Thornton are free and then handed them the papers granting them their freedom.

"I'm a free man. Master give us permission to leave the plantation. We be resting, then we leave here," Jacque further explained.

"A man traveling like you is in danger. We think you're runaways," said the patrollers threateningly.

"No sir, we ain't runaways, we free," Jacque insisted confusedly

"We can't take your word for it," informed the patrollers. It's our duty to find runaways and return them to the plantation they belong."

The thought of being returned to the plantation ignited dread in Jacque. He did not know what to say or think to prove to the patrollers that he was a free man.

"Jacque, who those men," asked Willa noticing his despair. Jacque turned to Willa gravely and replied: "They want to take us back to the plantation.

"Plantation! You a free man, Jacque. They patrollers," Willa questioned frightfully. Jacque did not have to reply for Willa noticed his despair and realized they had been captured by patrollers.

"But the papers, Jacque, you show them the papers master give you?"

"I don't know where they are," he divulged.

"Willa's heart raced with fear thinking about the possibility that if they were returned to the plantation, they could be separated. "But you had them, I saw you with them," she goaded insistently.

"That don't mean nothing if you don't have papers to prove you free," interrupted the patrollers. We have to take you back to the plantation."

Jacque and Willa were dispirited as they resigned to the fact that they had no choice but to be returned by the patrollers. Jacque attempted to console Willa: "We won't worry too much because master will give me new papers and I declare, we'll start this journey again." ..

Amalya and J'Nita were perplexed; they could not perceive Jacque in dream.; they could only see the patrollers approaching and accosting Jacque and his family. They were apprehensive about why they had appeared and what they would do. They observed with keen interest the confrontation. Their voices were inaudible; they could only perceive physical movement. When they saw the patrollers seize Jacque and his family, they were alarmed and wondered what would happen to them.

Back at the plantation, Jacque and Willa stood before Master Thornton. Jacque noticed his appearance was different and that confused him. He also sensed an atrocity lurking, but did not want to believe it was the end of his freedom or that Master Thornton had anything to do with it. He recollected the many years he deferred escaping for the promise Master Thornton had given his mother. The words reverberated as he stood before Master Thornton: "Your children will be manumitted." ... What had she died for, he wondered in despair. He was sure what took place. The master not only handed him his papers, but his siblings also, thus he was certain that he was a free man.

When Master Thornton addressed him, John became wary for his voice was different than before. He observed his manner as he listened intently.

"Jacque, you put yourself in jeopardy by running away," he began. Jacque's confusion mounted as the master explained, but he was not prepared to concede that he had committed a wrong. His hope was to remind Master Thornton about the proposition he made to his mother.

"You give me my freedom; I was hoping you would remember about those papers you give me when Mama died."

Master Thornton appeared indifferent to Jacque's explanation.

"Your Mama never knew any place else," he reminded Jacque.

"Yes, sir," Jacque agreed, "but ...

"There's punishment for slaves who runaway," interrupted Master Thornton. "I've given the patrollers instructions. You go with them now."

Willa bellowed plaintively and the infant began to scream. An urgent desperation possessed Jacque to try and convince Master Thornton what took place.

"Those papers you give me grant me a free man," Jacque pleaded, but Master Thornton turned away as the patrollers seized Jacque before he could finish. "I'm a free man, my children be free and their children," he reminded desperately. Jacque began to struggle to free himself from the patrollers. His pleading became louder and louder until the reverberations startled him to consciousness.

He looked at the empty space in bewilderment. A morning chill hung in the air. The child was crying; he was still torn between dream and reality. He arose with mild agitation and urgency and informed Willa: "We're leaving now; can't tarry in this place. We free and can't be slaves again."

"The baby is crying," said Willa helplessly.

"It's a long journey; that's to be expected," Jacque reminded her and began gathering and packing their things onto the wagon. Willa was hesitant as she was unable to comfort the infant. "I don't know why she's fretful."

"We must leave here if we mean to make our journey safe," he prompted.

Jacque reacted like a man driven by fear, fear he grappled to rid. Every action and thought brought him closer to probable rationality. He searched for the papers and found them; it was just a dream, he realized.

Willa noticed his malcontent and could not understand his sudden change.

"We don't have to worry about reaching safe, do we," she questioned.

"No," he replied confidently, "but we must leave now," he prompted.

Willa proceeded to join him to continue their journey. The child was quiet and Jacque had once again placed a barrier between his fears and the horizon before him. He possessed greater prospect than ever before as he proceeded.

Chapter 5

Crossing Boundaries

The day was growing bright. Every color imaginable sparkled in autumn's regal glory – orange glow of the sun, reds and yellows intruding the foliage, and scattering piles of brown leaves sprawled the sides of the road. Indian summer air stifled, seeping like a sultry summer day giving wonder about the advent of the season. Things unnoticed and unseen sizzled with life, like youth brazen with strength and endurance. The reviviscence of nature teemed vigorously.

Jacque pursued the horizon undaunted; the portent of peril having diminished. It was as if the dream never occurred or had vanished into thin air. The barrier of his determination was impenetrable and nothing could thwart it. Jacque was steadily casting away the miles between the plantation and his destination north. Nothing could impede him for he was no longer harnessed to a birthright. He was charged to do something with his freedom, like a Frederick Douglas, Nat Turner or Harriet Tubman. He couldn't explain the impetus of his thoughts, but all of his life he prayed and dreamed to journey north. The dreams about freedom persisted. He looked for freedom to appear any day like a star falling from the sky. He imagined all it had to do was rain down and he would be free. He held the notion that the star was so far away, it would take considerable time to reach him, but he dreamed and looked skyward and wondered when it might happen. Eventually, his dreams transformed to one who escaped to freedom running and running incessantly in the night only to wake up and find he had not escaped. He thought of the dreams he had as he traveled and knew it would recur time and time again until he lived out the true meaning of being a free man. Sometimes his dreams placed him in the midst of hordes of people, strangeness and strange places. When he awakened, he was not in fear, but in awe, because he was flitting with his future. Years of the recurring dreams, made him realize that one day he would reach north.

Often, the dreams would make him impatient and brooding. He loathed his predicament. Thoughts of escape gripped him. He then understood his siblings' actions – it was a difficult choice. He knew the dreams were prompting him to follow his siblings. One evening he enacted how he believed his siblings escaped. He couldn't rest as he lay listening for the quiet breathing of sleep from everyone in the cabin. When he felt it was safe to leave the cabin, he joined the still night and headed toward the dense forest. He was more frightened than he had ever been, for dreaming about escape was another matter. What lay in the midst of darkness was not an abolitionist or guiding hand, but things more mysterious. The brier patches ripped his clothes and mangled his skin reminding him of many perilous things, especially the danger lurking. He grew distressed and even more so when he realized his elopement led him to the river. He wanted to scream, but his hopelessness found no voice. The water did not ripple a silent and inviting flow, but bellowed angrily as if a storm was imminent. The clarion call of *return* guided him back to the plantation. He was shirtless when he crawled back to his padded space to rest. He couldn't rest, he could only think of the impossibility of what his siblings had accomplished. He thought and thought, but refused to admit defeat. There was something else, something more compelling, he realized. That dark night held his attention....

Now traveling north, a free man in the bright day, he could not easily forget, nor could he aptly believe the miraculous fact that he was journeying north. He was overwhelmed by what was taking place along with what was instilled in him all of this life about his dreams. He could not put to words the burden of his predicament and the source of his dreams, he only knew their sensory components made for trepidation and yearning and a telling to the individual. He exerted his courage to mask his fears once again because dreams like the ones he had were mysterious.

"How far north with going," Willa wanted to know, interrupting Jacque from his reverie.

"Trying to make it as far as this wagon can take us and we can stand the journey. Once we reach north, the first thing I'm going to do is affirm the legacy Mama left me. She left each of us a legacy."

He reached in his coat pocket and found another paper. He unfolded it to make certain it was the legacy. "You read it," he requested Willa.

She took the paper and scanned it briefly and then began to read: "Her words to you are" 'I believe you will be the son that will go astray like Henry, Ezekiel and Mandolin and, if you should leave the plantation, remember: The winds that stir up come from a mysterious place, move and change things all around us. We see the leaves fluttering and the branches swaying and sometimes trees are hewed to earth, but that doesn't mean things will remain that way. The winds will one day die down and maybe there will be gentle breezes and even stillness like peace on the earth; things will one day change.' Those are the words your Mama wrote you," said Willa returning the paper to Jacque.

Jacque did not want to stop at first, but hearing the legacy, it was now imperative he brought the wagon to a halt. He dropped the reins and took the paper and studied the words as if his mother was there reciting them anew. He had no voice, only inner thoughts and reverie about what he read. He realized slavery didn't make a difference to his mother's spirit, for she provided a way for him to set the words in memory and never forget the legacy.

Willa noticed how Jacque was affected by what he read. She knew freedom was always a yearning and burden to him. Many times they were together, he would spend hours trying to define it and grasp it. He desperately wanted to break the boundaries that prevented him from being who he was. She would worry fearfully when she saw him pace the earth intensely like he would escape that moment. He had no decision over his life and he harbored deep sentiments about his predicament. Willa believed that any day she would hear that he had escaped and she would be left unmatched and lonely. When that didn't occur and he became free through commitment and promise, it was an impossible dream come true. She felt the wagon pull ahead as Jacque took the reins. She saw he was still deep in thought and compelled to reach north and live as a free man.

"I'm grateful for the legacy," he finally commented and became silently thoughtful again.

"The end of slavery is near," Willa commented.

Jacque could not deny the present situation, but the future was still far away. Suddenly, Jacque grew wary and distracted for he believed he heard others along the road. He mentioned to Willa and she too could hear. Both of them noted alarm as they listened cautiously hoping it was the echo of the wagon on the desolate plain, but when that did not appear to be the situation, he realized intruders were approaching.

"They patrollers," Willa wanted to know.

"Can't say," Jacque replied as he slowed the wagon in anticipation. He was apprehensive as the portent of the dream reasserted. Inwardly, he attempted to buoy his courage: "It can't happen; it won't happen; it wasn't real; we can't go back; we can't be slaves again; we free." The words flowed effortlessly, driving away his despair.

Upon confronting the men, the contrariness of the dream was apparent. Instinctively, Jacque didn't believe they were patrollers, but caution made him guarded as he met them.

"You heading to the plantation," they asked.

Suppressing his fears, John managed to reply: "I think we're heading the same place."

"We're not sure if you are free or runaways, but that don't matter, we want to take you to safety. There are more soldiers and patrollers along this road than you can contend with," the strangers warned.

"Where's that," Jacque questioned.

"Not too far from this road," replied the strangers.

Jacques was apprehensive about the strangers' offer as the portent of the dream persisted.

"We haven't seen no soldiers or patrollers along this road so far; been traveling safe to our destination," Jacque explained.

"Don't know how long that will last. No harm to be safe," warned the strangers.

Jacque contemplated what it would mean if he refused their offer and encountered danger later. He would no doubt have regrets. Suddenly Willa diverted his attention: "I don't believe they mean to harm us; I believe they want to help us," she encouraged.

"I'm considering," he informed her. "They appear to be free citizens. The abolitionist worked through here long before the Yankees arrived. If they want to take us to safety, we go along. We'll be grateful if we're out of danger," he decided.

They followed the strangers to a sprawling tract of land several miles from the road. Most of the land was wilderness, unsettled by man, with clusters of trees and underbrush that made travel complicated. Jacque's skill at maneuvering the narrow passageways was tested, a misguided veer and they could overturn. Soon Jacque began to notice some well worn paths, probably beat down by the strangers to and fro in their travels. He noticed too, a plantation in his view and his heart sank for it reminded him what he fled from.

"Whoa, whoa," exclaimed Jacque suddenly.

The men looked back and stopped immediately. They stared at him in question: "Something the matter," they wanted to know;

John brought the wagon to a halt and looked around. The plantation he saw was vast land with farms, people and cabins. The similarity of the plantation persisted; he could not rid the thought of his former life and remained skeptical.

"What plantation is this," Jacque asked suspiciously

"This is where we live," the strangers informed him. Jacque and Willa reacted with disbelief. How could that be, they wondered. It was like it was a different place and time. Jacque could not decide anything; he could not go backward or forward; his reality was altered and his mind was seized with misgiving. Time had escaped him; he was in a kind of limbo. He knew he had the papers, the legacy and he was a free man, but beyond that it was like he was trapped in his former life. For an indeterminate time he stood remembering his family and the people he knew all of his life. It was like *déjà vu* but a different time. As he perceived the former place and people, even his mind was unlike a free man. It was not until the men offered him to stay for as long as he needed, that he became aware what he intended to do.

"I believe we are safe here," he finally realized

The strangers acceded with Jacque's decision. They escorted them to a cabin where they might settle down and rest. The strangers were optimistic about Jacque and his family thinking maybe they might decide to stay and become part of their way of life.

Beyond the corridors of the plantation, Jacque and Willa were able to observe life more closely. Everywhere they looked, work was being conducted by the farmers. Bales of cotton were piled high in large sacks on wagons; the thrashing of hay sounded like the wind whipping across the plain; the bleating sound of livestock being shepherded by farmers gave voice to some ancient will of guiding hands.

"Doesn't look like strife been here," Willa commented.

"I declare, if this be what's happening in these territories, my siblings in for real changes."

"This isn't the plantation we left; all these places are different," Willa reminded.

"I suspect the soldiers and the abolitionists have a lot to do with it. They intend to get us as much freedom as they can."

"You thinking to turn back," Willa asked.

Jacque pondered the question and the well of possibilities. He began to reminisce about what had taken place and what he had endured. Images of his former life were prevalent: the cabin, where he was born and grew to be a determined, sturdy man, laboring in the fields each day; his courageous mother and siblings; the reminders of the past were the steel binding links that gave him yearning.

"Drawn to our birthplace is as natural as breathing, but I don't mean to turn back. We're going ahead," he said decisively. "We should rest now; we have a long journey before we reach north."

They inspected the empty cabin; two small square rooms, a place to cook and washroom. They decided on the front section with windows, where light illuminated the dreariness of the room. They lay down their bundles and blankets and rested an undisturbed sleep, obscured by any worries they might have had. They were a family of hundreds who had taken refuge; who had circuitously outwitted their pursuers. . Those fleeing from slavery found a respite from peril for the path to the Underground Railroad did not begin at its threshold. Many families sheltered in places like they rested before crossing over to freedom. It was an arduous and difficult journey for the ones that had stopped over. Jacque could claim freedom, but they could not.

Jacque settled his mind knowing that he was safe and among those who had yearned for freedom and who had very likely gained freedom because of their courageous actions. Jacque rested like he was on a continuous ride down a winding trail; nothing interrupted him for a very long distance. In his sleep he edged toward the horizon which was sparkling with vibrant life. Every image of dream was enacted perfectly. The workers singing as harvest was being conducted, the grains pouring and being shuttled away. The roar of distance and freedom kept disturbances and fears away. The tranquility of another life inundated his existence so that the time of day changed from early morning to the sun approaching the horizon and a blinding glare awakening Jacque before sunset.

He looked around the mysterious space and wondered where he was. His mind was in a stupor and uncertainty. It was presently incomprehensible that he would be in such a place. Lucidity came slowly as his previous actions and encounters recurred. He remembered the rumble of approaching strangers. He glanced at Willa and the infant and felt safer. He arose and walked towards the door, opened it and saw the sun edging towards the horizon. He was on the plantation the strangers had escorted him, he recalled more coherently where he was. People were still working in the fields. It was harvest and he understood why the day had not ended for them. Sentiment and yearning arose; for him, harvest was the yielding of extraordinary things and it was always during harvest that freedom compelled him to unforeseen hope. The sowing of what he envisioned was never more real to him than during harvest. He gazed at what lay ahead until his eyes glared like the glow of the sun. So engrossed was he in thought, that he did not notice the approaching stranger who brought them to the plantation until he caught an extended friendly gesture.

Still somewhat dazed, Jacque gripped his hand firmly. "Much obliged for your help. We're traveling far and a little rest goes a long way."

"You join the bands of people passing through here headed north," the stranger reassured.

"I hope to reach there like them," Jacque commented as he observed the stranger for the first time. His skin was rugged like sandpaper from many hours spent outdoors. He had a sturdy, muscular build, and his clear sharp eyes held a purpose.

"I don't mean to discourage you," said the stranger, "You're a free man and can follow your mind. The law is coming to end slavery, but many plantations going against it."

"I see the problems and the dilemmas," commented Jacque.

"You hear tell of the promise," probed the stranger.

Jacque didn't know what to think of the stranger's question. He only wanted to stop-over and then continue his journey, but he obliged the stranger through consideration of his well-intended benevolence and replied: "I hear tell of a lot of things, but I go with the promise in my heart."

"There's no guarantee the promise be where you going," the stranger cautioned Jacque.

"I believe there will be opportunities and I'll take my chances," Jacque said resolutely.

"In a strange world like you might encounter, there will be dangers," warned the strangers.

"I intend to do some exploring to find out what a free man is," said Jacque adamantly.

The stranger recognized the determination Jacque possessed, but knew illusions were insubstantial and could change. He wanted to show Jacque the bountiful land that could be his promise also. No one knew better than he did since he was once an indentured servant who had worked until he became a free man over a decade ago.

"Before the miles tear you away, look around here and get in your mind what you are leaving," the stranger advised.

Jacque was sure the man standing before him was once a slave, but he rode horses and galloped across the land like a free man. *What manner of men are partners of destiny,* Jacque wondered. How long had he been free? Jacque searched his eyes and surmised the man was in his prime. A man in his prime has many horizons, he thought. "You mean for us to stay here," Jacque asked.

"If it accommodates you," replied the stranger and then commenced to guide Jacque around the plantation to interest him to remain and take up sharecropping.

"We had a promise and started as sharecroppers," informed the stranger as they walked.

"Sharecropping," John reiterated curiously.

"That's right and owner if that's what you want."

"I've been on this land all my life, it's easy for a man like me to settle here. This time of year you understand the promises has been fulfilled. It's an appealing offer; a man has to give long and hard consideration about it, but I'm just passing through on my journey north."

"Makes no difference, you know the land."

"No, I know the soil grows the fruit of our labor," commented Jacque tersely and looking towards the horizon.

"This could be an opportunity to build on a new hope and reap the promise. It's the birthright you can rediscover; I would like to think that's what a free man can do."

"I see you've lived through your doubts and promises. Freedom has just come to us and we are still searching. A man's has to feel free," Jacque explained.

"You consider I plow this land and wait on it season after season. There be good things and otherwise, but I'm an ordinary man against the earth and just want you to realize what an ordinary man like myself and you, can accomplish."

"You make a powerful proposition, cause a man to consider," Jacque admitted.

"If it is your choice, you can stay here on this land," offered the stranger hopefully.

John surveyed the land and held a deep regard for it. Sharing in the promise as the stranger proposed was compelling, but his mind was settled. "When a man's vision drives him, no telling how far he goes to fulfill it," he decided.

The stranger understood his resolve and had seen it from many travelers passing through headed in other directions, but he still made the offer available to Jacque. "If you change your mind, the opportunity is here," the stranger insisted.

"I'm obliged for your consideration and help," said Jacque gratefully.

The stranger did not escort Jacque back to the cabin but gave him directions and then bid him farewell. He watched the stranger walk towards a gully and disappear. He held a high regard for the stranger's courage and vision. Jacque felt the barriers vanishing by prospects of the offer of the stranger and the world which he immersed as a new horizon. As he headed back to the cabin, the new season was palpable and hung in the air like mist. He would remember this day, and maybe he would not return, but he would remember, he thought.

He noticed Willa standing in the doorway as he appeared.

"Are we in the midst of trouble here," she asked in a distraught manner.

"No trouble here, as far as I can tell," Jacque replied assuredly.

"Trouble comes when a man is between two worlds. One he was born in and dreamed all his days and nights that if ever he break free, he would go clear across the land as far as he can get from the world that denied him. Then by chance, he sees the very same world in a different place, at a different time, the soul begins to stir, unsettled by the new visions set before him. Freedom is changing this place, the land and people."

"We staying," Willa wanted to know.

"I think about what the stranger tell me, and I consider also what claimed my soul since I can remember. It's hard to deny the power of dreams. I have to see if my dreams be real," Jacque explained.

"The stranger must have given you much to consider," Willa surmised.

"I'll be considering until the second we leave," Jacque admitted.

Each day the spirit of harvest caused them to extend their stay. Jacque and Willa spent many evenings in celebration of the harvest. People assembled from the niches of the plantation, uninhibited and without restraints, no labors held them sway. Nights were like a comfort they had never known and the amicable ways of the people engaged their hopes and desires. Jacque and Willa joined the people who were not prone to long conversation but instead spent time tearing the blind of the sun from their eyes, and the toil from their bones by giving the earth a new jig and the evening a different face. They made bonfires that soared like dragons' fiery jaws. Jacque and Willa were enchanted by the people and joined hands to encircle the rhythmic flames. They sang and danced and ignited their nocturnal spirits to sublime superfluity.

It appeared to Amalya and J'Nita that Jacque and Willa had arrived at their destination and were celebrating the end of a weary journey. It was not until they saw Jacque and Willa depart at dawn, that they realized they were continuing north. They watched the wagon steered by Jacque move in unsteady rhythms as if it would cease to be the way they would reach their destination. They began to wonder if something had happened or would happen any second. They were anxious with anticipation as they followed Jacque and his family on their journey.

Chapter 6

Barriers and Battlefields

Jacque had to readjust his directions, for the warning of the strangers pervaded his thoughts and he became more guarded and vigilant. He stopped several times to avoid danger and confrontation with soldiers or patrollers. He did all within his power to elude any possible peril. He traveled different hours of the day; he hid in the wilderness covering the wagon, himself and family until he felt safe to travel again. Many days he was speechless and merely bound by his instincts and searching like a wary animal single minded and probing.

The days grew more frigid and sometimes it rained. Vivid autumn colors dissipated into dark verdure. As days wore on, autumn's beauty lay strewn in paths. Jacque was reminded of the season approaching. He had to reach north very soon. What kept Jacque determined was the vision of a free land and the dream haven he envisioned all of his life. He forged ahead gallantly like a soldier, mindful of the promises of winning the battle. I'm a free man, he kept reminding himself as danger insinuated unforeseen. He possessed in his mind memories of stories he had heard about hundreds of slaves who had run for freedom, inspiring stories that kept him hopeful that he would do the same. In his mind he carefully delineated his scheme, the one he devised many nights where he would lash out like a man driven by fate. He would overcome the obstacles before him and forge ahead.

What he devised was as vivid and compelling presently as it was then. Getting captured never entered his mind. In his scheme, after avoiding the dangers and withstanding the hardships, he would cross the line to freedom just like the hundreds of slaves he had heard about that found freedom. He would then connect to the abolitionists and the Underground Railroad in his pursuit. He remembered hearing about all the courageous and enduring men and women who had done great deeds for the cause of slavery by helping hundreds of other slaves become free. Those stories circulated over and over again in his mind and were the pulling strength to his determination to persevere.

The journey was so rigorous that sometimes Jacque thought he would faint or the reins would slip from his hands and his journey would end in a strange place. All around nature seemed to displace what had gone before reminding him of the advent of another season. There was already a chill in the air and hint of what was to come. At present, his mind seemed to flux between despair and hope. Why did he leave the plantation; why didn't he accept the stranger's offer? His taut nerves and questioning mind were fraught with anguish, the kind one feels when in the midst of desolation. He was like a man agonized by an unknown cause. His dreams taunted him; his fears raced through his mind but, he could not turn back, he knew he would not turn back, yet, the stranger's offer was a compelling proposition that disturbed what he had yearned for nearly all of his life. The conflict persisted as he traveled.

The journey became more hazardous than Jacque had prepared for. He encountered more battlegrounds and roaming militia than he could contend with, a reminder of what the stranger had warned him about and a source of desperation to avoid that fate. He and his family would not suffer that ordeal, he was determined. Sometimes, he thought he was traveling backward, he had changed directions and trails so often to elude oncoming dangers, became confused as to whether he was heading north. At night, he looked at the immeasurable firmament, in search of the north star, that guiding light that assured every traveling slave of where they were bound, and could not detect it, but he pursued in spite of his despair of not discovering it.

Flashes of gun fire where battles were being waged sent him plunging into trenches until he felt safe to continue his journey. During this time, he could not discern what was happening, whether it was reality or part of the harrowing nightmares he experienced at various times. The long journey was taking its toll upon Jacque. All the commotion around him was ominous and he didn't know what would happen to him and his family.

During sleep, the battles being fought disturbed him. The horizon darkened, obscured by thick clouds of smoke from cannons and gun fire. In his deepest despair, he questioned his fate for he realized that slavery was a hard fought battle, and the physicality of it was dreadful. It was like he was on the battlefield draped in uniform and observing the fallen dead bodies, blood pouring from the arteries. The specters of death made him groan in his sleep disturbing Willa and the infant who would scream uncontrollably. On many occasions, they had to cover the infant with layers of blankets to muffle the sounds. When he returned to sleep it was one continuous excursion through battlefields of death and destruction, up mountains, through valleys, everywhere battles for and against slavery spread and still Jacque managed to pursue steadily northward with images of decaying bodies, fallen limbs and bloody streams. Having been the percipient of such strange things and unspeakable events, he was overwhelmed by change, by design and purpose.

He began to realize that it was impossible even absurd that he and his family didn't perish right in the midst of their pursuit. He felt certain that by now he was headed for death; it was just a matter of time that gun fire would capture him, his dreams and future. Every night the visions of death prevailed until he decided not to sleep, not to visit dead visions of lifeless bodies. He willed insomnia upon him; no sleep, no death, no dreams; just awake, cast away the dead bodies from the trenches, but every time more dead bodies in trenches appeared all around him like sprays of gun fire. He was numb from anger, from disillusionment, from hoping and thinking that he could flee.

Amalya and J'Nita watched their ancestors in the midst of turmoil and confusion; wandering through a wilderness, lost and hopeless; they didn't know if they would find their direction. They yearned to help them in some way but couldn't; they peered hopelessly and bewildered nearly regretting what they had done for the thought of seeing their ancestors perish before them was harrowing. They felt trouble as their hearts and minds plummeted. They urged within not to see their ancestors perish before them.

When Jacque realized he had to journey through marshes and swamps or risk being captured, he stopped in despair. How could he? How, he wondered. He looked around unmoving and unthinking and then stepped into the soft earth like quicksand and conceded necessity. The mud and mire slowed him considerably as he waded through with his family. For days, he crossed wetlands trying to reach the other side away from peril. He prayed like never before, beseeching there be no alligator, no snake no unknown threat or animal. He wondered about the thousands of slaves who had escaped; he wondered about his siblings and if they outlived the treacherous swamps. During this ordeal, gun fire cackled in the air, howls of anguish ripped through every fiber of his being, he could feel the rumbling like an earthquake; death haunted him like prey; made him think insignificantly in the midst of everything perpetuating and teeming throughout.

When he reached the other side to dry land, he was frozen and still; his mind was vacant and worn. Before long, the only thing that threatened him was his illness; an ague attacked his being; he was like a violent man uncontrollable and bellowing. Disease fraught, some amoeba had come to carry him away, had elevated his body to a feverish condition, convulsed and rattling. Willa gazed in horror. She didn't know what to say or do. She had never seen anything like it. She only thought of death for Jacque looked like he was dying; she didn't recognize him; his eyes looked like a madman; his skin ashen; he was incoherent and he didn't seem to recognize her. She held the infant limpidly, not knowing what would happen. She looked around at stagnation; she heard animals in the bush and booms of gun fire, but they were in battle, maybe it was better to die on the battlefield. Would she be left alone with the infant in the wilderness, she wondered frightfully.

Jacque appeared to be getting worse. Willa did what she could. She found things; things that seemed to come to her for the moment to try and help Jacque and ease his pain. Through desperation, she was a being enacting the effects of what was supposed to be done in spite of not knowing what would happen. She comforted the infant to remain silent until she could put compresses on Jacque to relax his convulsions and to bring rationality to his mind. It didn't help right away; she discouragingly thought it wasn't helping at all. Spewing black bile from his torso made Willa cower in fear, Jacque was dying; only death could bring forth that excrement. Willa turned away and held the infant. She didn't want her near death too. The infant became silent during the ordeal, Willa felt her pulse to make certain she was alive and not feverish also. She seemed to be fine, she reassured herself. Jacque continued to expel excrement and Willa continued to look afar not wanting to face the inevitable. He looked like a different man, not the young, energetic, driven man she met a few short years ago, that took her on a whirlwind of imagination and dream of being free. He attracted her dire hopes and made her believe one day their lives would change. She was an orphan, but no slave was really an orphan, her mother was sold and she had to let go her apron strings and began work in the kitchen and there she remained until she met Jacque carrying water from the well and he assisted her; from that point they were together; destined for each other.

When his freedom was given, he was her knight in shining armor and no one could deny her. When they drove away, she didn't look back, she put up a barrier and the world which she had lived vanished that's when she knew what freedom meant. Now in the predicament she found herself, she was lost again; lost and searching, unknowing and beginning to lose hope. She got sticks and held them like a shovel and began to dig   Any thought that placed her in the midst of slavery, she repelled. She was as a child having made a grim discovery. the monster was an enormous ogre looking menacing down at her deciding how she would be mangled and torn to pieces like meat; and she would be carted away writhing and screaming mercilessly and unheard to human ears. Chunks of her would be annihilated and she would salvage what she could, but always tattered pieces would be left and stared back at her disfigured and bruised, like annealed metal, one part hot the other part cold so that if anyone touched her they would feel the same burning sensation not knowing whether it was hot or cold; just burning. She dug fiercely for she knew the inevitable neared.

Jacque continued to spew forth violently and raging in attack. She was in despair as the hole became wider and deeper. All through the day she heard gun fire and unseen animals and remained frightened she would be captured. If they appeared, a hungry animal or stray bullet, she did know what she would do, her life would probably end. She prayed they would not appear and harm them. She heard soldiers talking and planning; maybe they were deciding to apprehend them; it was nothing she could do. She stared in the direction of Jacque; his condition had not changed; he was now throwing away his garments. She turned away; it was awful. The baby slept as if it were a log; waiting to be moved, only then would she awakened it seemed.

Evening was approaching, but how could she sleep; sleep only came through desperation because the mind and body must travel in and out of consciousness that's human nature – to bring relief and solace; but Willa was troubled in either body; she couldn't discern whether she was sleep or wake her mind was in profound anguish. She fought frantically not to be carried away, and when it seemed she was losing the battle, she abruptly awakened to a dark midnight under the sky with hardly any sound or movement. Jacque was somehow sleep and unmoving at this time, or maybe she was dreaming she wanted Jacque to be sleep, peaceful and well. In any event it was a terrible quiet, in the unknown space where she felt any moment she would be captured; she wanted it to be daylight so at least she could see.

She searched for the horizon or any illumination that might bring her comfort. Suddenly there was a crack of fire in the air, red, orange and white that made her cringe with fear. It was so unexpected she felt her heart jump out and thought she would lose consciousness. She heard screaming and running and some times it approached very close to them. Maybe they would be ambushed; she was terrified by the thought and nearly stopped breathing so as not to be discovered. It was a war after all. Freedom did not come easily. Any moment, she realized that Jacque's dream could end; that they could be destroyed; that their journey north could come to an abrupt halt. Why did she not think of this before she left the plantation ... No! she had to be with Jacque. She could never forget. That was settled. Sometimes she heard quick snaps of twigs by heavy steps crushing them; and sometimes she heard silent snaps of twigs by stealthy steps breaking them and desperately entreated that no one would discover them. All through the night the sounds of terror provoked her and she steadily watched and wondered what would happen.

When the dark lightened and dawn neared, Willa moved quietly to where she was digging, found the makeshift shovel and began to dig furiously like it was the last thing on earth she would do; it wasn't the matter of digging but that she would not see, think or hear, no senses coming toward her; wanting to be in a kind of limbo. The area became deeper and wider and she achieved indifference and when the violent shove knocked her off her moorings, she was appalled and had to gather herself, lifting herself up from the moist earth and gazing in a kind of despair. It was Jacque; he was up, virtually nude and urinating where she had labored.

"Jacque," she screamed, but he did not answer immediately. She didn't know if he was well or sick. She only noticed the white light of dawn and suddenly the screaming of the infant impelled her. The infant responded immediately to her consoling. She feed her and changed her and comforted her and she was quiet. All the while Jacque was gathering himself; he was in a daze, he knew he had experienced something like never before – death neared. He looked around at where they had camped; he would never have stopped there; he couldn't recollect how he got there. He noticed it was a battleground. He sensed the danger and moved quickly to leave.

"We have to leave now," he commanded urgently. Willa was slow to react. She examined him closely to see his state of mind and if the sickness had subsided. He moved frantically and without hesitation. Steadily observing him, Willa began to believe Jacque had returned to normal; he was moving so swiftly that only a healthy and well person was capable of doing. She gradually became convinced that Jacque had overcome his illness.

"We're headed north," he urged. She proceeded to accompany him without reservation; thinking back when she had joined him and, together they left the plantation. The creaking wagon moved them securely away from the camp and battleground.

Within a few short miles, they heard canon and gun fire booming loudly in the air and realized for certain that they had left one of the many battlegrounds in South Carolina.

They skirted other areas where the armies were waging skirmishes as the civil war had become a full scale battle. The fierceness of slavery and antislavery clashed unyieldingly. Jacque constantly maneuvered to avoid many of the terrifying encounters that might prevent him from reaching the north safely. Along the river, in tidal basins and swamps, hundreds of soldiers on the union and confederate sides formed garrisons in defense of their position. Jacque had not calculated from where he sat on the plantation that he would run head on into the civil war. He knew, however, that once he neared the Mason Dixon line that he would be safe; that he would not have to hideout in the trenches as often and divert oncoming herds of soldiers, running and fighting desperately in battle. The paths were treacherous and sometimes Jacque was inundated with misgiving, but he forged ahead and remembered in prayer and the verses of clarity that would mean he was out of harms way:

> *Dark and thorny is the path.*
> *Where the pilgrim makes his way;*
> *But beyond this vale of sorrow,*
> *Lies the fields of endless days.*

For it was lore that many slaves found their freedom in such a way embroiled in an arduous journey of uncertainty, but Jacque and his family were some of the thousand who would crossover.

As they neared the northern territory, danger and threat diminished. Jacque began to notice a change in the landscape. There were less skirmishes and infantrymen ready to disarm them. Jacque was now more compelled to think about the place he would settle and build a new life and reap the promise. "I'm a free man," he kept reminding himself and as soon as he asserted his freedom, he noticed riders driving at a fast pace towards them and became tensed with caution as he had on many occasions traveling north.

"Are they patrollers," asked Willa noticing men approaching. Both Jacque and Willa held their caution and dread in anticipation of some unwarranted trouble they had avoided until presently, but when the riders neither stopped for inquiry nor uttered a word as they rode a fast pace away from them, both Jacque and Willa breathed a sigh of relief.

"I believe we're in free territory for sure," Jacque began to reason. "We've traveled many miles and it must be where we reached.

Chapter 7

Situated North

They had reached north, but continued to travel until their bones could no longer stand the grinding and rugged paths. Finally, John halted the wagon and announced: "This is where we're settling. I'll make my peace about Mama's legacy to me. 'I don't know what will happen, but we're here in the north, whatever is our destiny, we'll see it through."…

They had arrived in Manhattan weary but spirited. The city had a way of life and activity they had never seen. People looked hurried and frantic as they walked. Some steered wagons and fancy carriages around the closely constructed buildings that towered towards the sky. Both Jacque and Willa were so overwhelmed by the strangeness they did not know what to do or where to turn. Gradually, Jacque surveyed the surroundings to decide which direction to pursue an inquiry.

"We facing trouble," Willa wondered somewhat repelled by the strange environment.

"In a different way, I expect, but nothing that can't be worked out. If we find a place before sunset, it will be our beginning, Jacque replied.

For hours, it seemed an endless and futile search, but Jacque was determined to settle in the city. He remained calm and observant. Eventually, they were driven to a section that was mostly colored people. Jacque stopped the wagon. He tried to put his dreams before him, but the images that compelled him to leave the plantation were unrecognizable. He turned away from his dreams which seemed, for the immediate circumstance, undefined. His eyes steadily searched for something familiar in the crowded and strange avenues. From the plantation, he hadn't imagined such ornate spaces, things and people filling up and overflowing into congestion. Finally, he noticed places people were entering and leaving freely and decided to inquire. As he drew closer, he began to decipher what his eyes rested upon: *"Antislavery Society"* sprawled on an oversized billboard. Once it occurred to him what it might be, he was impelled forward. "I think I see a place," he murmured with uncertainty.

Jacque brushed the dust from his clothes, straightened his hat and stepped down from the wagon to investigate. As he walked, he checked to make certain he had the papers. The closer he got the more fearful he became, but he could not turn back now. He was conscious of the air, his breathing and the strangeness of the city. The storefronts clamored with activity; people passing by and sometimes stopping for talk and laughter. Standing in front of the building, Jacque studied the surroundings with a reigning mood of doubt, but found the courage to open the door and enter. His presence distracted an unassuming looking man sitting across the counter. Jacque noticed the man was very much a northerner, highly curious of who walked across the doors of the Society. Jacque knew he had scrutinized him the second he looked up. In an instant the man had probably pinpointed exactly where he was from. As time proceeded, Jacque's observation would prove entirely correct as it was the business of the Society to help alien and distressed slaves who had crossed the Mason Dixon with their predicament to adjust to habitable areas like uptown Manhattan.

The man stood up and walked to the counter where Jacque stood. They were now face to face. The man had immediately decided Jacque's fate. He was salvageable and could be accommodated, for Jacque had a presence about him that was amiable to the man. Jacque only had to rid the barrier that prevailed that made him appear alien. Impeded by his predicament, his mind fled backwards, as the man scrutinized him.

"You from around here," the man asked to make certain.

Jacque could not respond, but the man surmised the answer and next asked: "How can we help you?"

Jacque's thoughts began to unravel, but he was still agitated and appeared confused. "I ... uh ... I'm a free man just arrived here," Jacque managed to utter nervously.

"Well, how can we help,' the man probed.

"I have my papers to show I'm a free man," Jacque continued as he offered the man the document to examine. The man received the document offered by Jacque and skimmed it with compelling interest. He had seen many documents and could detect forgeries. The paper was a heavy parchment used for formal documents; that was the first indication to the man of its authenticity. He next noticed the alignment of the words was carefully set and the master's signature could not possibly be duplicated. He finally determined the document was authentic and returned it to Jacque.

"That's a valuable document you possess; you should keep it in a safe place. Slavery will be ending, but you can't tell what might happen in the meantime. We're here to help runaways, but you're already free."

"That's right," Jacque said talking through his fear and uncertainty. "This is the place I find my freedom. I just arrived here and ... well," ... Beads of sweat began to form across Jacque's face; he wasn't certain what to plea since he was already a free man. He hesitated and wavered in thought.

"You want to settle here," asked the man trying to help Jacque through his difficulty.

"Yes, I need to settle here," Jacque responded nervously.

"Do you know of any relatives who might live here," inquired the man.

Immediately Jacque thought of his siblings who had run away. They could be in this place, he realized. But, he didn't have a trace of their whereabouts, he reflected skeptically. "I don't know where they are," he finally responded.

"Many slaves who arrive north, change their names and that's why it's hard to locate them," explained the man as he examined Jacque's reaction.

"Then you might be able to lend us a hand," Jacque asked anxiously, not wanting to be turned away and desirous of the need to settle in the north.

The man stared at Jacque as he had hundreds of fleeing slaves who found their way to the society. Very few of them were free like Jacque and he wasn't sure what he could do, but some things occurred to him that might benefit Jacque and the Society.

As the man contemplated, Jacque sensed dejection in his uncertain condition and quickly rallied to convince the man to assist him.

"I may be a free man, but my freedom is just beginning. I've come a long way to reap the rights of freedom. I intend to stay free."

"Your name," asked the man.

The question took Jacque by surprise. He hesitated momentarily before he replied: "My name?"

"Yes, we need to know your name before we can do anything," informed the man.

"My name is Jacque Thornton," he said nervously and feeling the interrogation was a preliminary he wasn't used to. He didn't know how much more he could withstand, but he was in dire need of direction.

"Well, Jacque Thornton, we'll do what we can to help you stay in the city. We can use supporters like you. Will you join us?"

Jacque wasn't sure what to say and what the interviewer meant, but stuttered a reply: .... uh ... I don't know ... I intend ... yes," Jacque finally decided.

Most slaves we help are runaways scarred of body and frightened for their lives, but you hold impressive documents. The man hesitated as if searching for the right words to convey to Jacque. He understood that even though Jacque was a free man, there were other obstacles he faced.

Jacque stood restive and concerned about the future. His mind was transfixed on the question of what would become of him now that he had reached the north? His yearning and hope momentarily descended to misgiving, but he withstood all manner of dissent that would deny him. The voice of freedom urged him forward: "I'll reap the promise of a free citizen," he was finally encouraged. Jacque returned to listening to the man as he spoke.

"Mr. Thornton, every place here is not safe, you must understand that first. Many slaves have had the misfortune of being caught and returned," the man explained as a warning to Jacque about what could happen. "I think I can recommend a place where you can settle. This place is for free slaves like you and won't be any problems with runaways. You travel alone", he asked.

Jacque was so immersed in the persistent thoughts of being turned away and the time he was a slave and the time freedom haunted him like the sun on his back, the rain pouring down, the river meeting streams and the fields expanding before him, that he was momentarily speechless.

"You travel alone," the interviewer asked again.

Finally, Jacque responded: "No sir, I have my wife and child with me."

"That's fine with us. I'm going to recommend a place and give you directions. Are you a reading man?"

"I read a little. You show me a map and I follow it," Jacque replied.

"This place is far from here, but I don't think you'll have trouble finding it, once I give you directions."

The echo of freedom was presently greater as John watched the man write the directions. It had taken nearly his lifetime from the time he realized he was a slave, to reach this moment. When the man handed him the paper with directions, he attempted to examine the sprawl, but his vision was blurred from overwhelming emotions. "You say this be a safe place," he asked in a barely audible voice.

"Indeed, no fear of runaways. I suspect once you reach there, you'll agree," replied the man and then proceeded to explain the directions to Jacque.

"I'm a weary traveler by now," said Jacque once he comprehended the directions, "but I'll see my way through."

"You settle in, just remember we can use a man like you here at the Society. Be looking to see you soon," the man reminded Jacque.

"Can't forget the offer," said Jacque as he extended his hand in gratitude before walking out the door. He was now more anxious than ever to inform Willa about their good fortune.

This was the beginning of Jacque's experience with freedom in the north. As he walked through the door, the man scrutinized him as he had done hundreds of others who sought help from the Society. From his personal investigation, he was prone to draw his opinions and conclusions.

"I can tell a man pursuing a dream, I think he'll do well here," he decided.

The change in Jacque's manner was apparent to Willa as she watched him approach. Her patience had spent but she remained reticent until Jacque climbed onto the wagon staring in the direction of the Society. He didn't immediately divulge to Willa what happened like he thought he would. He had to sort things out. He felt like a bewildered and confused child. All through his life he wanted exactly what happened to him, and yet for the moment it was incomprehensible. He studied where the Society was located for he intended to return.

"I have to remember where this place is, it's our beginning and maybe it's our future. We're on our way to settle in a place."

Jacque said everything Willa hoped and prayed for. She sat silently rejoicing as they headed in the direction given by the man.

Jacque was careful to make every turn and follow every road precisely as the man instructed. As they drove through the streets, the bright sun made everything visible and noticeable to them. They were seeing the area in its entirety; the people were many and diverse laboring with bundles strapped and carried from place to place. People exchanged products and other merchandise in the markets. Life in the north far exceeded what Jacque and Willa imagined. Jacque was inspired by the many prospects that lay before him.

"I'll be returning to the Society," he reiterated as if more certain about his decision.

"They give you work," Willa asked.

"It's more than work. They help runaways be free once they arrive in the north. We're not runaways, we free already, but they helped us too," Jacque replied.

"What work will you do?"

"I'm not sure, but I think its part of what I need to do. Dreams don't always come as you see them," Jacque explained.

"You see all these people and places around us," Willa observed.

"This is the right place for dreams, no matter what happens there's always a promise on the horizon."

With their sense of hope restored, they became preoccupied with the vastly different way of life which reminded them how far they had journeyed from the plantation. As they traveled, their spirits became driven apart from the labor and toil under the sun and instead embraced the strange streets and pathways as they searched for a place to settle. The clearly designed buildings, the precise curves and winding streets with people meandering conveyed the possibilities of life bustling before them.

The entire time Jacque drove, he glanced at the directions constantly checking to make certain he was following them accurately. The farther he drove the more he was reminded how different the north was, the people, the streets, the density; instead of space there were things, different and unusual things. He especially noticed people strolling, talking and examining wares in the marketplace under the yellow sun that sometimes created looming shadows that never seemed to go away. Jacque began to establish a sense of time and space about where he was presently. He looked out at the vast and changing horizon; a light flickered as the day began to change. Just enough sun to show evening approaching he noticed.   The buildings were more spread apart and desolation suddenly appeared causing Willa to suddenly ask out of concern: "

"We nearing the place?"

"We nearing the place for sure; the map and directions agree. I believe we might watch the first sunset and think of the new days ahead," Jacque replied with assurance.

"There's a lot to see and learn about the city. I don't know how long it will take us to know the north; it's like we're invisible to the eyes we meet," commented Willa.

"Maybe it don't make a difference that we just riding through this place and then again, maybe they riding for the same reason," said Jacque. His voice lowered noticeably as he approached a building. He checked it against the directions he was given and then exclaimed: "I declare, we've reached another destination!"

Both of them inspected the outside of the building with curious interest. It was similar to the ones throughout the city: wide in structure and ascended skyward with levels of glass windows that glinted from the evening sun. But, no amount of time observing the building could help them get used to its unusual appearance for it was a remarkable contrast to anything they had imagined or seen.

"Is that the place we might stay," asked Willa.

"I followed the directions and this is where they lead us. I go and inquire to find out," Jacque replied.

He walked up to the large wooden door and knocked persistently. The sounds reverberated in the quiet, still air. He noticed darkness descending as he waited and thought of being turned away. He anxiously surmised what might be occurring that caused the delay: there was no one there; they recognized he was a stranger or the man had misguided him. No, he reasoned as he checked the directions once again. He was at the exact location. He knocked again and within seconds, a portly man opened the door disarming Jacque for several seconds. The man, clad in a suit and an inquiring stare, observed Jacque with suspicion and wonder.

Jacque, aware of his scrutiny straightened his shoulders to appear more guarded before speaking. "Evening sir," Jacque began. "I'm ... uh ... Jacque Thornton. I came by way of the ... uh ... Antislavery Society. I was recommended; I'm a free man." Jacque noticed the indifferent stare of the man and was momentarily speechless.

"*Free*," questioned the man dubiously.

"Yes sir," said Jacque confidently as he removed the papers from his coat and handed them to him. The man accepted the papers and read them carefully. What he read impressed him. Seldom did slaves appear fully emancipated like Jacque and with documents. After scanning the contents, he was inclined to accept the document as proof of what Jacque informed him about. He returned the papers to Jacque and presently held a different view of Jacque.

"I'm Rev. Goodwin," he introduced himself.

"Glad to make your acquaintance," Jacque acknowledged.

"Those are impressive papers you hold," commented Rev. Goodwin.

"Got me this far sir," said Jacque.

"You come this far to settle your freedom, Mr. … uh …" The reverend was trying to remember Jacque's name and looked at him for help.

"Jacque Thornton," he reminded the reverend. "I always wanted to travel north.

Rev. Goodwin nodded an understanding and then explained: "I don't know if what's here is fitting for you."

Jacque searched momentarily and suddenly remembered the message from the man at the Antislavery Society. "This is what I was told to show you," Jacque said as he handed the reverend a sealed note.

Rev. Goodwin reacted as if he expected to receive such a note from Jacque. He unfolded it in a decorous manner and read it. Like the man at the society, he was used to many people appearing at the door wanting help or a place to stay. The society helped him decide who might or might not cause trouble.

"Well now, this is how you got here?"

"Yes sir, they give me directions and I follow them. Didn't have trouble reaching here.

Rev. Goodwin was convinced Jacque was a *bona fide* free slave and decided to do whatever he could to help him. "I must check on a few things first; can't say what's available yet."

"I'll be obliged to wait, sir. I journey a long way and can use a place to rest," commented Jacque.

"I understand. I see what I can do," said Rev. Goodwin before leaving.

Jacque walked over to Willa to inform her what the reverend intended to do. "We're settling here I believe," he said confidently.

"That's promising," Willa said in relief. "Night coming and I hope we'll rest soon."

"I believe we will," Jacque assured her. We wait to hear from the reverend. There are more people than I ever imagined moving free like us that don't seem to have to worry about anything but their dreams," Jacque observed. As he spoke, Willa noticed the reverend had returned and informed him.

"This is the time of day we need to know we can settle in a place. I go to hear what the reverend has for us." Uncertainty loomed as Jacque hurriedly proceeded to learn what the reverend intended for them. As Jacque approached the reverend, he surmised, cautiously, that he would not be turned away. When the reverend began to explain what he could recommend, Jacque's doubts waned.

"You know space here for slaves is a problem. There's not enough places for all who come here."

"Yes sir, this is just a beginning," Jacque commented anxiously.

"Well, seeing you realize that, it'll go a long way in understanding what can happen. We don't expect trouble, but we have had our share. We like to help every slave and those papers granting you a free man we consider highly. What we recommend is a small place, but it's all we have. It's not far from here if you're willing to consider it."

"Jacque felt his body rattling and unnerving in tingling sensation as the burden he had carried all of his life moved. He could barely restrain his emotions from the overwhelming feelings that inundated him. "I'll be grateful to settle in as soon as I can," the words escaped from him like an echo.

"Since you willing, I give you directions ... uh ... Mr. ...."

"Mr. Thornton," Jacque reminded him.

"Mr. Thornton, this place is not far from here. Follow in that direction," he pointed to show Jacque where he would be headed. "You want to get there before dark."

"I'm thankful," said Jacque reverently.

Rev. Goodwin scrutinized Jacque again and then commented: "I believe you might find your way in this city." It's not an easy place to live, but I think you'll do just fine," was the reverend's final assessment before they shook hands and departed. Jacque watched Rev. Goodwin return inside and then walked briskly away with an exorbitant feeling of triumph.

"Willa," he called excitedly as soon as he came within reasonable distance where she could hear him, "We're settling here before sunset."

"We settling here," she checked to make certain she heard him correctly.

"The place is up the road, and evening won't find us wandering," Jacque informed her.

"We've found a little hope after all," said Willa. "I was wondering if we would. I declare, tonight our dreams will be in a free land. I imagine it will be hard to wake up."

Evening was settling over the city in a grey, dark pall causing the buildings and environment to appear desolate. The activity and attractions had dwindled. The sidewalks were emptied of people and only had remnants of boxes and debris strewn along them. The strangeness of the city was more perceptible creating in Jacque a dire urgency to find the place the reverend recommended.

The distance was shorter in comparison to where they traveled from the Society. With evening approaching, it was more difficult for Jacque to discern where he was. Emotions of uncertainty began to disarm him as he traveled, but he remained determined. He examined the direction and studied the area unerringly until he located the building the reverend recommended.

"Cabins are different in the north," Willa observed.

"We can't expect nothing like the plantation we left," Jacque reminded her and, in the same moment, noticed the building the reverend directed them.

"This is the place," he announced excitedly. He halted the wagon and both of them stared at the closely knit structure and thought about how it would be shelter for months or even years. They pursued many possibilities until Jacque was prompted to inquire.

He stepped down from the wagon and walked a few yards to the entrance of the building and knocked persistently until the proprietor appeared. The proprietor did not delay and was straightforward in asking Jacque if he was looking for a place to stay. Jacque explained how he arrived at the building to the satisfaction of the proprietor.

"I see, I see," the proprietor commented as Jacque stared at him not knowing what he would do next but hoping he would accommodate him with a place to stay.

"We must be careful about strangers and runaway slaves. If the reverend sent you, you already have a night's stay and for as long as you need. You travel alone?"

"No sir, I have my wife and child with me," Jacque replied.

"Well, this is a small place, but you might manage."

"I'll be grateful to settle in before evening," Jacque commented.

The proprietor did not delay in escorting Jacque to the place he had for him. Jacque possessed one solitary thought as he followed the proprietor and did not notice the several other places that were lined with recessed doors shut tightly as if uninviting. The hallways were empty; there were no porches or verandas to hold conversation or lean against to ponder illusions. In time, Jacque would learn that northerners did not leave doors open, and were most often guarded and not prone to acquaintance and conversation.

After a reasonable walk down halls and up flights of stairs, they stopped in front of the place that would be available to Jacque and his family. The proprietor searched through a ring of keys until he found the one belonging to the door. He uttered a sigh of relief upon locating the key to the door. He unlocked the door and invited Jacque to inspect the space.

"This place has bed, dresser, chair and window. If this be to your liking, you can settle here," the proprietor informed Jacque.

"Sir, we travel a long way to reach north, we need a place to stay," was Jacque's way of saying he wanted the place. They spent several moments working out the details and conditions of tenancy. It was Jacque's first time encountering such formalities, so he was careful to understand what he was getting into. After they agreed to the arrangements about tenancy, the proprietor gave Jacque the keys and left him to further inspect the dwelling. Jacque was tangled with emotions like he had never known. It never occurred to him that he would feel outwitted by his fortune. Jacque stared vacantly like in a state of shock and disbelief about the surroundings. He thought of his mother and siblings and still he could not belief what was happening. He did not know at what point his mobility returned, but he knew he had to inform Willa eagerly where they would be settling, and left eagerly.

"Step down from the wagon and see what we have," he directed Willa. It's small, but it's our beginning; this is our place for now. We're settling here for whatever it's worth. Reverend say space for slaves is scarce in the north, so we have to remember that." With child in arms, Willa followed Jacque towards the building.

The closed doors, long hallways and steep stairs were strange and unusual to Willa. There was some resistance from the unknown, and she did not immediately favor the new environment, but she believed Jacque had secured the best dwelling for them.

Jacque sensed her reaction and was quick to assure her. "This is where free slaves like us stay. Ain't no runaways. Those papers master give us allows us to be here," he commented. Willa began to feel a little more at ease, as Jacque explained. When they finally reached the door to the unit, Jacque hesitated in order to prepare her for what she could expect.

"Remember, this is our beginning. It's not a cabin, but a dwelling like northerners are used to. I show you our place." He opened the door for Willa to see what he could not explain. She regarded the livable space reverently. She saw promise and hope and all of the things Jacque talked about, she began to realize.

Jacque saw that Willa didn't mind the space and was settled with what they had found. "I expect we'll be here for a while," he informed her.

"Don't mind if we do. North is coming to mean freedom and a little space too," Willa commented as she decided how she would embellish the rooms.

"We can settle now," John prompted. It's just about dusk and we'll be dreaming with the northern stars above us." We'll go and get out things.

Before they left, they walked over to the window and noticed evening approaching and darkening the buildings nearby. The northern sunset made an auspicious beginning and gave them more prospect and determination It was a mysterious view to them, far from the plantation, cabins and fields; it was like they were watching a rainbow; something they expected but didn't know they would actually see. Their anticipation was high as their spirits soared. They could have remained relishing the moment for an eternity but they had to move everything from the wagon to the unit before dark. It was the last thing for them to do before the glow of the horizon reminded them of their dreams and weariness.

When the sun had descended completely, darkness appeared in a midnight blue and a few lamps in the street glimmered a glow like fireflies. It reminded them of how far they had journeyed. With promise of a new life, they were soon consoled and rested peacefully.

Not once did the child whimper, nor were they disturbed by any untoward thing. Their sleep extended like eternity and denied anything that would disturb them. Their freedom became actions enacted in dreams; illusions as if they were awake. They were greeted and welcomed by people; they were given novelties they had never seen before. They went down winding roads and traveled along tracks and rode on trolleys which drove them to the end of the city. They looked at the river that did not bar them from freedom and saw enormous ships and people coming from the depths of the water. Freedom was everywhere like they had envisioned the north would be.

They revisited the society for it had its influence on Jacque especially. Its benevolence and great prospects aroused in Jacque an urgency that compelled him to enter the door of the society. The incessant sound of a bell pealed louder and louder, disturbing and agitating him like danger. He wondered about the man and thought he would wait until he appeared, but the pealing sound became like a siren echoing unbearably. By sheer will, he bolted forward as if he had been catapulted by a machine. He was disoriented and perplexed by the mysterious surroundings. Dazed, he looked around the strange room and wondered why he was there. The inordinate hours of sleep seemed to have obscured his memory. He searched for evidence in the room. Gradually, thoughts began to evolve. Slave. Free. The two worlds juxtaposed in his mind. Free, he remembered he was free. He glanced around and saw Willa and his daughter who were still resting soundly. It was not a dream, he realized. He looked at the items of furniture and recalled the proprietor. Slowly, lucidity was returning. He followed the light emitting from the window and saw the new land.

Daylight in the city was vibrant. Buildings appeared taller and sturdier with perfectly aligned brick from length to breadth. His mind followed the infinite immensity. It was strange not seeing field, farm, cabin and workers. Strange not being without but contained in one of the northern dwellings. His thoughts went beyond the small dwelling and into conjecture about the city. How could he reap the promise? When he was a slave, he could see it vividly. Now, in the midst of his dreams, a free man in a free land with many things to pursue, he wondered where to begin. His mind probed and probed the possibilities. He began to feel downcast and reverted to pessimism. Despair seeped in making him somber and disturbed. He realized he had only done work as a slave; that was his dilemma: he didn't know what else he could do. It would take time to adjust and learn the ways of the city. Where should he began, he questioned as he looked at the looming horizon and beyond. Apprehension gripped him as he felt alienated from everything he ever hoped. His dreams were as remote as the miles he had traveled. . How could he forget? For the moment, he felt his dreams had been vanquished. The urging of a new beginning was as palpable as the sun that propelled the world forward. He saw men harnessing their wagons and horses and going about their way in wonder and defiance of what might prevent them from living or pursuing their dreams. They moved like gentle beasts away from the world that contained their dreams into a world that would outlast any imaginable thing that they fathomed. The north has its way with men's dreams, he realized. The avenues and horizon did not just form its distance but the possibilities of reaching and exploring. Jacque had to find his way. Whatever fear poking at his consciousness had to be ridden.

He immersed his will in the new world glinting so fresh and promising. He held his stare, unafraid and thinking of his dreams that were filled with a complexity that still captivated him with yearning and possibility. He tried to revive the pristine mornings where, like his forbearance of time, that inspired him to go beyond. He affirmed and reaffirmed what was proposed and never heard the knock at the door believing it part of the specters and nightmares beseeching him asunder. Instead, he continued to hear the pleading voices guiding him to his destiny, but the knocking persisted.

"Jacque, someone's knocking at the door," Willa urgently informed him. Immobile, he stared in the direction of the door; the intermittent silence made him disbelieve. Another loud knock startled him to wonder who it might be. He walked hurriedly towards the door and opened it without hesitation. It was Rev Goodwin standing neatly suited and possessed of a purpose so compelling he did not hesitate to inform Jacque.

"If you rested by now, you might want to consider this place of work," Rev Goodwin informed Jacque. Jacque stood dazed and speechless. A shadow cast over him like weariness. The words were slow in penetrating.

"You must reply now," prompted Rev Goodwin. Jacque didn't know exactly what Rev Goodwin was demanding of him, but he noticed his impetuous manner and thought it best to respond. "Reverend, I'm obliged.

"This is work you can do. You're a sturdy main suited for it; it's dock work by the river. Don't expect no trouble, because you're a free citizen and have your papers in case," the reverend explained.

The ambivalent feelings Jacque experienced upon awakening began to vanish. He began to comprehend that the reverend was offering him his first opportunity for labor in the north. "Rev Goodwin, you say this place is near the river," Jacque asked to make certain.

"Yes," Rev Goodwin assured. "Ships and boats come to the harbor from all over the world. It's an advantage the city has being surrounded by a river. Ships sail in the harbor bringing products of all kinds.

Convinced, Jacque was now anxious to pursue the offer made by Rev Goodwin. He wondered if he would be able to find his way to the river as he studied the directions. Rev Goodwin instructed him how to proceed before he departed. Jacque was immersed in reverie once again as he stood against the door listening to Rev Goodwin descend the stairs. When his footsteps faded and it seemed he had departed, Jacque thought momentarily about the good samaritan who offered him a helping hand and made it possible for him and his family to walk the path of free life in the land of his dreams. He would learn the ways of the city, its customs and maybe some of the people, he decided.

"I'm going to the river for work," he announced to Willa, seeing that she was fully aware but possessed with a look of concern.

"This town doesn't look like it has a river," she commented incredulously.

"Manhattan is a big island surrounded by water. The reverend say ships come here from all over the world and bring things and people also. I'll be doing some kind of work on the docks; I'll find out when I get there.

"Goodness, Jacque," Willa exclaimed still in disbelief.

Jacque sat in a chair near the bed where Willa was sitting with the infant. He looked at his daughter and noticed she was growing and changing. Presently, she was wide-eyed and curious, turning her head as infants do when they are alerted. Her dark bright eyes searched the room and noticed both Jacque and Willa and then she lay her head with coiling tresses against Willa's shoulder. Jacque showed a knowing smile; his daughter resembled the Thornton's. Viola Mae was his mother's name and he would always be reminded of his mother through his daughter.

"Today, I looked out and wondered what would become of my dreams. Then the reverend offered me them first promise. I'm going to the river as a free man and see the ships coming and going in the harbor.

***

The first day Jacque reported for work at the docks, he was carried through a rigorous procedure that was so grueling that he was on the verge of fleeing for fear he would be taken captive. He had to see a foreman first before anything was considered. The foreman was located in one of the ships which he later learned was a different ship at any given time and very few people knew which one he would be boarded for he changed from ship to shore to dock and was very elusive.

When Jacque boarded the ship, he felt his body tense and the strain nearly impeded his mobility. Being on a vast ship like the one anchored in the Hudson River was ancient and remote to Jacque causing him to feel he was in another world and time. The steel railings encasing the exterior like a fence, the cabins and especially the dimension of the decks were equivalent to city blocks, the vertical masts, the billowy sails, the helms and periscopes imposed upon Jacque like a great tide thrusting him ashore so that when he reached the compact office of the foreman in the bottom of the ship, he was senseless and he didn't know what to think or how to react. He was inundated with emotions that made him apprehensive about what might happen to him as he confronted the foreman.

The foreman, a white man with sea-tanned skin, sandy hair and alert eyes attempted to allay his apparent distress. He immediately proceeded with the formalities. The recommendation from Rev Goodwin was regarded highly and Jacque was ordered to report to work the next day.

Thereafter, Jacque worked all day on the docks moving cargo from enormous ships that came from thousands of miles away. Sometimes he would gaze outward as they approached the harbor and imagine the different places they had sailed.. The brilliant reflections simmering on the surface of the water bespoke untold lore of seafaring places, places that were beyond his grasp and dreams, but there he was vicariously experiencing the promise and remembering the river down home was a long tributary he couldn't cross, but the river in the city he could begin building his dreams.

Chapter 8

Fulfilling a Mission

Amalya and J'Nita were again surround by darkness, staring into an abyss, fearful when the light faded, but mindful not to make the slightest movement that might cause reversion. They didn't know how long they would remain in the lurch as they waited for time, light and images. They thought of what they had seen and were eager to experience more of the history of their ancestors.

Time spent inconspicuously into years during which Jacque and his family adapted to the city, the people and way of life. They gradually settled in as citizens and, unless you knew them previously, you could not tell they were anyone but northerners. . It was far from the life on the plantation. Freedom allowed them to live a life they were denied before they reached north. They formed neighborly bonds with the people they lived around primarily because of Jacque's outgoing concern about the people and surroundings. Word spread that Jacque and his family were free citizens and the people realized the high significance placed on freedom.

Every day Jacque's dreams manifested in ways he imagined while still a slave. Jacque became known as an avid worker both on the docks and for the Antislavery Society. Jacque was one of the Society's most influential associates. He was proud to envision as world where there was freedom for everyone. Freedom was the call of the day. Emancipation had accelerated to the north, outward and beyond. Hundreds of slaves still appeared at the Society seeking help. How could he forget the plight and emotions on their weary faces? Jacque was compelled to assist in any way he could. Every time the trail of a runaway slave was thwarted so that no trace or evidence could be found, Jacque had engaged himself personally to achieve the results.

The man he met at the society upon his arrival in the north, he now knew as Mr. Smith. They had become confidantes and shared common purposes. Both of them were equally committed to achieving the goals of the Society. Mr. Smith provided him with many intimate details about the Underground Railroad that impressed upon Jacque how prodigious their services were. The Underground Railroad was an elusive entity many years ago, but currently Jacque was in the midst of its influence and was fully knowledgeable of the fact that the Underground Railroad was responsible for the freedom of the majority of slaves who fled the plantations. Often, Mr. Smith would pull him aside, lower his voice and begin explaining: "If it weren't for the Underground Railroad, many slaves would still be in bondage. It's a perilous mission we conduct. Intricate paths to freedom have been devised for slaves willing to risk their lives to gain freedom. Very few people know the exact routes many slaves have traveled to reach north, but the Underground Railroad is certain to have helped them find their way. When slaves come here, they are sworn to secrecy about how they arrived. We hear about Frederick Douglas and Harriet Tubman, but the majority of abolitionists don't want to be known; that's why we have to be careful with runaways, no telling who they are."

The more Jacque learned about the Society's mission, the more he acted with prudence and caution.

He was a conductor and the one responsible for leading slaves safely to freedom. Seldom did he encounter problems he could not resolve. On few occasions, he even traveled as far as the border of Canada where some of the runaways wanted to join family and friends who had gone to live in Canada. The patrollers had no right to reclaim fugitives once they reached Canada because it was a different country with different laws and slaves were treated differently.

The first time Jacque traveled upstate towards the Canadian border, he saw fields and farms that reminded him of the plantation back home. At first he was caught off-guard by the expansive territories and landscapes that resembled his home, but with every mile and every person he encountered, he began to feel the difference in place and the influence of freedom upon that land. He understood the mission of the Society and his purpose. Near the Canadian border, he would stand and watch the runaways cross the barricade separating one country from the other and marvel at the thin line between freedom and slavery. When the runaways finally touched soil, they were greeted openly by supporters and abolitionists. Each time Jacque witnessed the sight of slaves becoming free citizens, it affirmed to him the significance of his mission. He would watch until they disappeared into safety. He could have remained indefinitely witnessing the remarkable occasion because it reminded him time and time again what he yearned for all of his life. It was hard for him to tear himself away, but when he did, the return journey was fraught with visions of the many who found freedom.

Over a period of years, Jacque had personally helped to free many slaves, effectively carrying out the mission of the Society. Eventually, the day would come when the proponents of freedom would convince the government that emancipation was the only resolution for those in bondage. The idea of emancipation began to grip the land and more conflict arose between north and south. As slavery neared an end, the opposing forces contested their wills. The abolitionists and masters defined and refuted the laws for slavery and freedom. Neither would go quietly into the night until it persuaded the government to take a final stand. And it did, but not without bloodshed and the virulence of opposition and conflict.

On the brink of emancipation, the Society became involved in one of the most controversial situations ever. A family who had reached north, later found their freedom in jeopardy. The mission of the Society was to secure the family's freedom permanently. Jacque was appointed by the Society to plea for the family's freedom.

For days, the mission for which he was obligated plagued him. It wasn't that he doubted the Society's position; he believed freedom belonged to every person, but some unsettling thoughts about slavery lingered. Freedom was every citizen's right, he kept thinking and trying to rid the effects of what he lived most of his life.

He considered the way in which he would present the matter before the tribunal. His utmost concern was that the family remain free and in the north if they desired. "No law could make them slaves again," he insisted. It was a guiding principle as he reviewed every aspect of the case. There grew in him a mild sense of contempt for those southern states that avoided the emancipation laws. He contemplated if the tribunal would consider the old laws of slavery which gave slave owners rights to dispose of their chattel as they saw fit. The very idea incited both ire and futility in him. In spite of the unwarranted feelings and the conflicting laws, he remained determined to continue the Society's objectives. How slave owners could win any favor was a mystery to him, but it was happening. It was senseless to him that emancipation was the law but slavery remained. Freedom will prevail, he reasserted as he pondered the strategy he could devise to allow the family to remain free.

Many evenings found him solitarily thrashing out his position in defense of the family. No one could disturb him during those moments. Willa and the children were virtually invisible to Jacque. Willa knew how important it was to Jacque to complete the work for the Society. Jacque recognized Willa's consideration and held a tacit promise that things would return to normal once he won freedom for the family.

Jacque took every opportunity to fulfill his mission by hinging his plea on his long held convictions about freedom. He thought about when he was a slave, the plantation, his family and his long held dream of being a free man. He contemplated every possibility; a man with freedom and a man without freedom are not the same. He lived both; that family was his family searching and reaching as if they were destined to climb a mountain that was arduous and fraught with many perils. It was a risky voyage, but they would not turn back; they would not descend into the pitfalls of misgiving. Freedom was every person's right.

Jacque took pencil to paper and wrote the plea for the family. He let his newly found freedom be his guide. He felt the unburdening of slavery and was assured as he wrote what would help the family remain in the north. From dusk to dawn the specters of slavery haunted him and drove him on the brink of despair. He heard his parents' voices and nearly faltered and turned away for he realized they were never free but their dire hope for their children propelled him forward and he proceeded undaunted by any fears. The clarion call for freedom was forever embedded in his memory. The family for which he pleaded was every family caught in the clinking chains of bondage. Free alas, the dusky horizon seemed to beckon. He looked, as if from a lofty height, and descried the entire universe from the mountain on which he stood. Freedom was every person's right. The Society's mission would be accomplished, he insisted.

After many hours, when he was assured that he had fully expounded his position, Jacque buried his head in his hands thinking of the days ahead and beyond, weighing each possibility and outcome, but there was only one the Society stood for. Even with emancipation being the law, there were rights owing to the south that troubled him. What would happen if those rights prevailed and the family was returned to the master according to the laws of disposition granted slave owners. He stared like into a void not wanting to think about defeat. He remembered the day he became free, it was bitter/sweet, there were propositions, the inevitable occurred, he became free.

That day held him captivated; his mother's strength and wisdom as she bade them farewell one last time. He would never forget. He was reminded of his birth place, his siblings and his long absence. He thought about how far he had come; the mere fact of working through his promise was bewildering to him; even though he believed it might happen, he wasn't sure how. He thought of his other siblings, the ones who ran for freedom and realized they probably found it. He didn't want to believe they had perished. He wondered if he would ever see them or worse, that maybe he had seen them and didn't recognize them and they did not recognize him. He understood their triumph was different and one he could not share. He didn't want to be like them for their disappearance was still uncertain. He could not bare the thought for it especially reminded him of his mother's despair.

The overwhelming thoughts brought back profound memories of his life on the plantation and he was urged to write his siblings at the homestead. He searched for the information he had on the papers Master Thornton had given him and thus he began writing his siblings. Distant memories came to the fore and he began writing as if he had communicated with them constantly. The years swirled, as he explained his travels and works; recollecting their conversations about what his life was like in the north. The memories that had been stored and waiting for the precise moment he now rendered were clear and defining. He envisioned his mother, the field and labor and reproved himself for desiring to forget everything about his former life. It took him a long time to compose the letter as there was much to relate about his experiences in the north.

As he wrote, he wondered if all of his siblings were alive and well and still on the plantation and how the effects of emancipation had spread throughout the region. He was now in high anticipation. He was anxious to send the letter to his siblings and to receive communication from them. He felt he had been remiss for not having written them sooner. He felt qualms as he carefully composed his explanation. He imagined each sibling as their faces came to mind, but he knew, like emancipation, they had also changed, but it was the spirit that was the same, the never-changing connection of kinship that was common to every family. The man-child was listening to the past and it was like the song "Freedom" he sang at home and in the field that echoed all around. It sounded differently like the hymn song to the spirit that ignited hope again. By the time he finished the letter, his trepidations had alleviated and he felt confident that the letter would be well received by his siblings and they would eventually reply.

* * *

Freedom teemed on the Thornton homestead like the slaves could never have imagined. Many mornings, after emancipation was formally proclaimed, the former slaves congregated around the plantation entrance to hear what might happen to them. The former slaves were anxious to learn about their future. During this time, each slave became a person searching for a common solution to their fate When the word "slave" was dismantled and sharecropper offered instead, it sounded new and impressive and, of course, it was a remarkable change for them. For the slaves who became sharecroppers, the sun seemed to shine a different light; their burdens were different as they began to comprehend the difference between slavery and freedom. What transpired because of emancipation transformed the plantation like never before and created incredible impressions in the minds of the former slaves who remained.

All of Jacque's siblings decided to remain on the homestead. They believed in the promise of a new life on the plantation and witnessed the changes taking place throughout the region. Elijah and Samuel had already been sharecroppers and were settled on the idea along with Emily and Leona. The proclamation was just a reminder to them of greater freedom for all. Their neighbors were now more understanding of the lot they had experienced years before emancipation. They were no longer held in contempt or suspicion because they were granted their freedom. They could never explain to the satisfaction of their neighbors why they were granted their freedom and the others were slaves. Their friendship waned considerably among the neighbors the day Master Thornton fulfilled the promise he made to their mother. Now, with emancipation that had changed; sorrows were set aside and celebration for a new day and life was replaced. The plantation was now a homestead for all who remained. What was once a place and conflict and suspicion had now become a neighborly land.

Emily and Leona were relieved and unburdened when they saw their neighbors' reaction. When freedom possessed their neighbors greater than slavery could claim them, it made a significant difference. Many mornings Emily and Leona would hold conversations about what had taken place. They would sit in the pantry off from the kitchen, facing the window and watch the new day begin and reminisce time and time again about the events that changed their lives.

"It's been our deepest yearning for every slave to be free like us," Emily began.
"I dreamed about it more than I can count. When emancipation was proclaimed, the plantation was thrown into upheaval. I never seen anything like it; the scurrying didn't stop until those who wanted to be here were settled and those who wanted to leave disappeared."

"New and different people came here to," added Leona. It's not the same place, but who could expect that, when Lincoln set down the law freeing all slaves in the land."

"It was like we celebrated all over again," Emily smiled joyously as she remembered the day it happened.

"Yes, we did," commented Leona. "It's nothing wrong with dreaming. I always prayed for this day. The funny thing now is we have to wonder what's up the road for freedom."

With freedom, no telling what may come our way," commented Leona.. We're in Georgia and we have to consider what's happening here. Already, we have witnessed more changes than our eyes and minds can handle. All of the changes and new people coming and going, it's hard to sort things out." "It's different now," both of them agreed as they stared through the window wondering what the day held in store. Many days found them bewildered, they didn't know what to make of all the commotion. They had to rely on Samuel and Elijah for guidance. Both Samuel and Elijah had come into their own. They had wife and children. They were mature, grown men who took on the task of freedom and change like necessity. Sometimes Leona and Emily didn't recognize them and had to sit back and wonder where the rambunctious and spiny boys had gone.

"In the midst of all that is taking place, I was thinking about Jacque. I'm like Mama, I guess, admitted Emily. There's not a day that goes by that I don't think about him. You know Mama was like that we Mandolin, Ezekiel and Henry. I come to understand that when you make a pie and put it out on the table and pieces are missing, it's not whole anymore. If Jacque could have waited just a little longer, it would have made a world of difference."

"No, no," said Leona, "Jacque didn't believe in freedom here"

"I declare, Jacque went the way of the other siblings. We haven't heard a word from him either. I can't help from wondering whether he's dead or alive, safe or harmed," complained Emily. I think of him as being out in the strange world lost; but I know he's not lost, because Jacque wouldn't allow that to happen, but we haven't heard from him and I can't help but wonder."

"We knew when Jacque left that would be the situation, but what I would give to hear a word from him," Leona yearned. "Time has brought change and I believe if he could see this place now, he would consider returning."

Suddenly a ringing of a bell startled them, causing them to stare in wonder at each other and them in the direction of the sound.

"It's too early to hear that," Leona reasoned.

"Master Thornton warned us to expect the unusual," reminded Emily.

"The important thing he said is that we would get wages for our duties," commented Leona.

"That be the bell again; can't be mistaken this time," Emily urged.

"I'll go and see about it right away," Leona prompted.

Alone, Emily's thoughts were about Jacque; recalling the day he rode away from the plantation in their father's old wagon creaking stiffly, but finally starting his journey. She regretted his departure, but it was nothing she could say or do to convince him to stay; none of them could convince him to remain on the homestead. Jacque had prayed and planned for the day all of his life; nothing was going to prevent him from pursuing his dreams.

Emily sighed from the realization that the south had faded from him like water evaporating. He wanted to forget his former life and start anew. She couldn't hold it against him, Emily reasoned, for he kept his promise to their mother.

Emily was faraway in thought when Leona returned waving an envelope anxiously. The gesturing distracted her and caused her to wonder why Leona was so agitated.

"What's the matter," asked Emily. Leona didn't answer. Emily watched her gaze at the envelope like doom. She didn't know why she was acting so strangely. All sorts of thoughts came to mind, but most of all she was fearful of what the envelope might contain. She had thoughts of her dreams and nightmares some more prophetic than others, but nonetheless potent for surmising what the envelope might contain. She recollected the time when Master Thornton handed her an envelope and she gasped for breath at what it contained, never discovering at that moment what it was , but waking up in another reality with considerable thought. Soon she realized Master Thornton was handing her freedom.

Presently, she had become less fearful and more prone to pursue other possibilities about the envelope. Leona remained silent, but Emily could no longer tolerate the mystery about the envelope.

"What is it," she wanted to know. This time, Leona glanced at her with suppressed vision as if she too was frightened by some nightmare or encounter that contained a portent about the envelope. Emily took control of the situation, believing whatever revelation, they had to know. She offered to take the envelope from Leona.

Finally, Leona found the voice and explained: "Master says this envelope is for us. There something in it, but I'm confused by what I see."

Emily turned it over and over, then held it up to the light where both of them could see the outline of its contents. She began to decipher the lettering and, as comprehension slowly set in, the meaning had struck like a new world had flashed before her, one she had imagined and yearned for. "It's from Jacque," she exclaimed as loudly as her voice could ascend startling Leona to joy and curiosity. "It reads: From: Jacque Thornton, …New York!" …

Leona clutched the letter again. "I don't remember seeing those words before," she admitted.

"Well, that's what it says and that's where Jacque is. Now we know he got that far and he's alive and well!"

"What is the meaning of it; I don't know what to think because something could be the matter with Jacque," Leona commented suspiciously.

Emily thought momentarily about the possibility Leona was concerned about. "We'll open it and find out," she prompted. She nervously opened the envelope and removed the contents. She unfolded the letter and confirmed it was in fact from Jacque. "It's Jacque's writing; I know his handwriting."

"What did he write," asked Leona impatiently.

"We'll read it and find out."

"You read it," Leona suggested and handed it to Emily.

Emily was anxious to learn its contents and readily took the papers and began reading:

Dear Siblings:

Time has a way of running its course and before you know it you find yourself in the midst of a new day. It was never intended that I should disappear without a word. I and my family (two girls and a boy now) made it safely to the north and are working out the dream and promise. This vast, new land is more than I can put into words. I have traveled a span of untold miles and still do not see an end in sight to the slavery problem, even with emancipation. I do service for the cause and see the intricacies of law and freedom for slaves and I'm committed to making emancipation an exemplary law. The turmoil of change can be seen throughout. Each state differs, but we aim to fight for the right of the law to free slaves throughout this land. I think of the Georgia plantation because it is our birthplace. I believe, as of this writing, my siblings, Elijah, Samuel, Emily and Leona are still there, if not, I'll be grateful to know. It is my earnest hope that emancipation has embraced you and not made you a stranger. I do not know my siblings' condition, but now we can say we join each other once again. If ever it be your hope to travel north, you will witness the spread of freedom. But, if freedom has uplifted you there, then we can continue to join hands, north and south, in emancipation. I dreamed this day and serve the cause of freedom.

Brother Jacque

Emily and Leona were speechless but groping for explanation. They peered into the open space and everything had a new meaning. They envisioned

Jacque in the north and sensed exhilaration with every thought. Emily exclaimed in amazement: "Three children!

"That letter brings Jacque from a million miles away," Leona added. "I declare, Jacque didn't forget us."

"How could he forget. I guess it's just a matter of time that he might look this way again," Emily commented hopefully.

"We can't do nothing but be glad that we now know Jacque's situation. We never expected it, but we know now and if we hear from the other siblings, well ... we wouldn't be able to put it in words. Emancipation is the law now, they must know they don't have to worry about patrollers; they can travel like free citizens."

"That would be the day to see all the siblings come home," Emily added.

"Like Mama, we won't give up hope about those other siblings," said Leona optimistically.

"Jacque mentioned he's working for freedom. Seems like he ran with freedom and is fighting for it also.

"Emancipation is law, what is he doing," Leona wondered.

Emily was now more proud of Jacque than ever for he proved to be very courageous and didn't let any predicament stand in the way of his beliefs. She could still see him and hear his deep voice singing about freedom.

"Many states differ like he says and maybe that's the problem. Jacque's in the midst of experiencing it and must know things we don't."

"Well, we can certainly rest better knowing about him and we can't forget to tell Elijah and Samuel;

it'll ease their worrying also. Both Emily and Leona were now both faraway envisioning what the north was like and what Jacque might be doing.

"Can't you just see Jacque up north fighting for freedom," commented Emily. "I don't expect he wears a uniform and carries a rifle like the Yankees, but people recognize a determined man when they see one."

Leona was inclined to agree and concluded: "I guess he was destined. "We'll consider everything he's doing for the cause of freedom. In time, freedom will be the spirit of the land because of men like Jacque Thornton fighting for it."

Chapter 9

Justice Prevails

Several nights Jacque had difficulty sleeping because of his concern about the outcome of the hearing and whether what he considered was sufficient for the family to remain free citizens. He had recurring nightmares of captivity and failure and constantly thought about the family and the extent to which he had to go to defend them.

After learning where the family was confined, Jacque decided to visit them. It was the same building the hearing was to take place and he knew how to get there. He had learned his way around the city and outlying territories since his arrival north and could find most places. Even with the fast pace of growth and expansion, he had become accustomed to the new way of life emerging like it was his birthplace. When he drove through the streets, people acknowledged him as one of the associates of the Society and helped him in any way they could. He knew now more than ever that the Society needed the support of the citizens and so did the family. How they would help, he wasn't sure, but as the hearing proceeded, their voices would be heard.

When he reached the building, he was recognized immediately and directed to where the family was sequestered. He could hear his heavy treading echoing down the lengthy corridors until he reached the area and stopped. He decided it was more discretionary to observe the family indirectly. From an alcove, he looked through a bay window and saw the family he had to defend huddled together in despair. There was no communication between them. They sat with bowed heads and silence. If Jacque had a way to their thoughts, he was certain the plantation loomed large in their minds. The cruel master still wanted to possess them and give them lashes as punishment for running away. Jacque was in deep thought about what he must do. He had to convince the tribunal that the side of justice was with emancipation and that the family's circumstances were unusual because they crossed the laws of slavery and emancipation. The pendulum swinging back and forth had both the past and future. Justice was on the side of family, Jacque reasoned, and the family must remain free. Jacque made his determination without confronting the family; he did not want to raise or put down their hopes prematurely.

The day of the hearing, roars and shouts from a horde of people in front of the building and surrounding area were evident when Jacque and Mr. Smith arrived. The spectacle encouraged their optimism that they would prevail and that justice was in favor of the family. Jacque hesitated and gazed at what was taking place before entering the building. Mr. Smith was more accustomed to the event and had to inform Jacque: "They're here to support the family in case they are made slaves again."

Jacque acknowledged Mr. Smith's comments and added: "What we witness is the hard fought battle for freedom. Seems like it don't make any difference what the law is, slavery rears up and haunts at every turn.

"That's why those people are out there to make certain the law don't go back. The law gives that family the right to be free" Mr. Smith added.

"Each of us realizes slavery is not far enough in history for us to stand in certainty. That family found every means to reach north and freedom; they risk everything, now their fate is in question. What is the proposition for the family to remain here," Jacque questioned.

Mr. Smith considered Jacque's concerns and the circumstances of the family. There was a dilemma. The Society's position was always the same – all slaves should be free citizens, but the south hadn't seen fit to recognize emancipation. The Yankees may have won the war, but the battle was still raging.

"It's hard to give up centuries of possessions. Some slaves don't know where to turn. Before long, we'll see more slaves just like that family in these corridors," Mr. Smith noted.

Jacque recalled the day he arrived north. He carried the papers granting him his freedom. He felt more proud than he could describe, but the family did not have papers and that made the prospect and what they could consider more complicated. He again contemplated how he would convince the panel to allow the family to remain free.

"That family crossed the laws of history. On one side there was slavery and on the other emancipation; one law pulling them back and the other law pulling them forward." The old south and new north are still in conflict. If we can convince the master to recognize emancipation, then that family will be free like the law gives them the right to be. The people gathered and waiting won't rest until this situation is resolved."

The crowd amassed along the street in support of freedom inspired Jacque and Mr. Smith not to be defeated as they scrutinized the realities of the family's fate.   They knew it was up to them to continue the Society's objectives and remain a beacon of hope for runaways seeking refuge.

"You know when the laws were written to govern this land, all of those rights owing to citizens were not intended for everyone."

Jacque did not have an opportunity to consider the fullest intent of Mr. Smith's comments for both of them were suddenly distracted by a commotion stirring among the crowd. They moved closer to the window and stared into the street. They then noticed three white men jostling their way through the frenzied crowd as they headed towards the building. At once, Jacque and Mr. Smith realized it was the master and officials arriving for the hearing.   Jacque was suddenly overwhelmed with doubt about what would happen to the family. Seeing the master walking intently reminded him that slavery still commanded the moment and the difficulty they faced in eradicating the southern way of life that had lasted centuries was more apparent.

"Brace yourself, Mr. Thornton. The deciding moment is upon us," Mr. Smith commented.

They watched the crowd's intense stares as the master and officials walked towards the building. Once they reached the entrance, Jacque and Mr. Smith decided it was time to join them in the room where the hearing was to be held.

They entered a large room with light emitting from the windows that faced the street. Long wooden tables and chairs were aligned across from the panel of judges situated at the front of the room.   The murmur of the crowd was still audible and permeated the room. Jacque glanced at the family he was to defend: mother, father and children sitting in the center of the room with heads lowered like their fate had already been decided.

He noticed the master and officials huddled in consultation and wondered what they might plead. He believed the law was in the family's favor and would be upheld. "If the law of emancipation differs in this situation, I think I am mistaken about the meaning of freedom," Jacque commented in a muted voice to Mr. Smith.

"Don't worry Mr. Thornton, this is just a formality. We won't be daunted by it; justice is on the side of emancipation.

Before they could venture into any other possibilities about the fate of the family, the sound of the gavel alerted them. They glanced in the direction of the panel that appeared austere and ready to render a final decision. Jacque's will and determination hardened as he stood steadfast in his convictions.

Words flowed from the panel of judges inspiring awe and rendering the room absolutely silent. Jacque listened intently for he was not certain if the words supported the Society, the family or the master. He contemplated inwardly as the formalities were pronounced. He would like to believe that emancipation was the order of the moment and that the family would proceed in freedom, but he was uncertain. Anxiety pervaded, but no sudden outbursts ensued. When the words were concluded, the room remained quiet like it was frozen in time. Then Jacque noticed the master rising from where he was seated having been called to give testimony by one of the judges.

He was a tall man and was conspicuously an outsider in demeanor and dress. An aura of another placed pervaded as he prepared to state his plea to the judges. When he began to speak, his voice represented a distinct southern drawl and wielded specific attention in spite of the new law. He was authoritative and persuasive when he spoke:

"Panel of judges, we've come to this northern territory to ask that justice be served and that every power of the law be used to see fit to return the family to the owners. That family is part of our right to fair disposition which brings us here today. These obligations are part of the truce between north and south and I present these papers as proof." The master produced papers which supported his statements and before delivering them to the panel, he reviewed them one final time.

Jacque and other members of the Society reacted dubiously and the crowd was heard murmuring in protest because they were not certain what the papers contained. Mr. Smith tried to quell the malcontent arising: "Those papers are in question and the panel must consider them." Their attention was again drawn to the master as he continued his plea.

"Emancipation freed slaves and that's the law now, but we have the right to resolve the previous law. We're not here to contest emancipation, but to exercise our right to disposition. If this family decides to return north after we rightfully decide our business about them, then it's entirely their decision. I request that this panel consider the truce, not only the emancipation law." Before he could finish his plea, protests arose from the crowd disrupting the hearing. It took several minutes before order could be restored and for the hearing to resume. The master grew silent, appearing affected by the uprising. All words and explanation that would have followed were omitted by him. He returned to his seat and regarded the panel of judges with consternation.

In the meantime, the panel reviewed the documents presented by the master as Jacque and Mr. Smith surmised what might happen. In their view, justice loomed and would be the order of the day, but the plantation and its influence still pervaded with the master determined to compel disposition like the family had no rights.

Jacque voiced his pessimism: "If that family is returned, it will be a terrible tragedy."

"Mr. Thornton, emancipation is in our favor," reminded Mr. Smith, but it was like his comments were unheard.

"There comes a time when life seems to stare back at you. It's a moment and lifetime where every action has led to a particular moment and you're obligated by a looming question: What should be done?"...

"They're waiting for us," Mr. Smith prompted.

Jacque startled briefly and then gathered as much courage as he possibly could because he understood that sometimes the greatest intentions could go awry. He was determined to persuade the panel to consider the Society's position as the only just and proper thing. His composure was stoical as he observed the indifferent panel waiting to hear his plea. When he spoke, his voice resonated clearly through the room:

"Panel of judges, I'm here as a representative of the Antislavery Society. You must know the Society is an organization established to help slaves who have arrived in these territories. The abolition of slavery is upon us because history has ruled on the side of freedom. Emancipation is written as law now and it will be a great injustice to this family to go against what is law. I stand before you as a witness. I was a former slave and now I am a free man who arrived north.

Freedom is a long and tireless journey; the miles that separate slavery and freedom are innumerable. That family is among the tens of thousands searching for a new life. They arrived here with the greatest hope of what can be attained in freedom. The master cannot, on this new day in history, deny that family's freedom. If disposition is what the master wants, we ask that it be done and settled in the north."

Jacque finished his plea in the midst of an open protest from the master and his officials. Jacque was not disarmed since he realized the master was determined to repossess the family and return them to the south. Jacque joined the other members of the Society whose confidence had mounted upon hearing his plea.

"You made a strong recommendation for that family," Mr. Smith encouraged. Why the master is resisting the idea can only mean slavery might linger a while longer for that family if they are returned. "I wonder if that panel intends to turn back history and rescind the freedom of that family."

Mr. Smith glanced at the panel scouring every detail and surmised what the outcome might be, as the panel gave no indication of preference. The family's situation was unique, but he believed a decision could be reached. The question loomed what the panel would decide. He viewed the master as an adversary of freedom and from a long line of slave owners who regarded southern law over the law of the land. Mr. Smith knew there was reason to have misgiving even with the new law.

"The master has produced documentation that's making a powerful impression on the panel, but emancipation is law and that's what we have to remember," Mr. Smith encouraged.

Waiting for the panel's decision was intolerable. Silence became fear and fear became skepticism. The master's confidence and composure were disarming. The men of the Society considered the possibility of defeat. What if the documents granted the master the right to return with the family? Then immediately as the thought of defeat proposed, the men of the Society dismissed the idea and insisted silently: "It can't be, they cannot rescind the family's freedom." They weighed their position with he new law. The moments seemed like hours as they searched inwardly the matters that had not been decided.

A stir was heard among the panel of judges, distracting Jacque and Mr. Smith. From what they observed, it was apparent a decision had finally been reached. Looking stoically in the direction of the panel, Jacque and the men of the Society braced themselves for the final judgment.

When the panel ordered the master and members of the Society to step forward, everyone readily conceded. The panel did not hesitate to set before them an unusual compromise to resolve the matter before them. When Jacque heard what it was, he reacted with disbelief.

"I never thought I would live to see the day we would have to purchase something that should never have had a price on it in the first place." Jacque was stunned beyond comprehension and began to voice his opposition to the panel, but Mr. Smith reminded him: "I know it doesn't seem proper, but that family isn't going to live in freedom if we protest. It's the Society's purpose to see every slave free. We will proceed from here, Mr. Thornton. You did what you could and it was a fine plea. History must stay its course. That family will remain here and live as free citizens as intended by the law."

By the end of the day, Jacque and the members of the Society were able to take the family into custody. Jacque looked into their eyes and the despair had vanished and in its place was optimism. Freedom was as real to them now as walking into the streets where the dispersing crowd was still pronouncing triumph. The unpleasant task of exchanging money for freedom, Jacque now considered in a different light along with other aspects of freedom and justice. He contemplated, as he walked through the corridors whether justice had been served and if there would be peace and justice in the pursuit of a better life with emancipation as law of the land? …

***

Amalya and J'Nita could no longer repress their elation at what they observed. Time can render another perspective and conclusion about anything thought to be impossible. What they discovered about the past rivaled everything imaginable.

Years of dreams and long dark nights sped through their lives and the yearning now resounding in triumph echoed in the cluttered attic. So forceful was their rejoicing, that the trance-like condition gave way, leaving them speechless and in wonder about what they had experienced. …

They looked around the attic trying to remember why they were there; they didn't recognize their surroundings immediately. The present seemed intangible as they began to sort out reality. They embraced each other for reassurance that they were not reincarnated; that they were who they had been in their memory. The looked around the attic and touched the objects once again; silently searching for distinction or revelation. It was not until Amalya saw the family record beneath the rockers that clarity illuminated. They remained stunned but their voices attempted to pronounce their experience as things were becoming more lucid.

"I won't forget, I won't forget," they uttered simultaneously. Amalya remained silently relishing the past as J'Nita continued to speak.

"I won't forget what I have learned about our ancestors and especially Grandpa Jacque Thornton. He was gallant in what he did for freedom by helping runaway slaves remain free up north. I can't believe the Society had to pay for that family's freedom," commented J'Nita and then looking at her mother for explanation.

Amalya understood her daughter's concern as she thought back to the time she questioned her grandmother about similar things. She searched her memory and could vaguely recall the history of the way slaves could become free citizens: the master could free them, but it was not always certain they would remain free, especially if they journeyed to other places; another way was through purchase like an indentured servant. One legend in particular she remembered and believed it might clarify J'Nita's concerns. Thus, Amalya ventured an explanation.

"During that time, it was common to purchase freedom for slaves and fugitives who arrived north. This was before emancipation. The most famous incident was that of James Hamlet. He was a fugitive who arrived in the north, but was later arrested and threatened to be returned to slavery. The abolitionist gathered together and eventually purchased his freedom. That's what I recall," said Amalya as she reflected on some other details about the past. J'Nita appeared to weigh every word with heightened fascination.

Is the Society still in existence today," J'Nita wanted to know.

"Those societies were founded to help abolish slavery and once emancipation became law, they went the way of history. But that is not to say the fight for the cause was over. After slavery was abolished, other organizations appeared for new causes."

"Did Grandpa Jacque join other organizations," J'nita wondered.

"I'm not sure" answered Amalya. "From what I understand, Grandpa Jacque was industrious and hard working and divided his time between the Society and his family. When emancipation became law, there was a lot of turmoil with the thousands of slaves migrating and trying to rebuild their lives. After the new law, leaders arose like Booker T. Washington, W.E. DuBois, and others.

"I remember reading about them," commented J'Nita. I even memorized some of the verses in Souls of Black Folk by W.E.B. DuBois. It's very memorable because I think it's kind of spiritual. The part I like is about the race being like a "seventh son," The verses came back to J'Nita almost instantly and she began to recite them aloud as fluently as if she were reading from the book. Amalya was captivated again by what she heard from J'Nita. She remembered when J'Nita first learned the verses and how inspired she was about learning the words. At first, she was like a fledgling uncertain of the meaning and had to read the words over and over again to establish her own perspective and understanding. When began to comprehend the thrust of the words, the intent and purpose, what manifested became her dream-like vision of another world and people. Amalya was impressed her daughter had not forgotten those verses and displayed appreciation for it was evident, as J'Nita recited, that the spirit of the words was connected in the past and the present.

"We have certainly come a long way," Amalya commented when J'Nita concluded. J'Nita smiled primly. Her yearning about the past was still apparent. There were other aspects she wanted to know and experience. How could she ask her mother if they could return to the past and see their ancestors once again?

"There's so much here," complained Amalya with mild frustration and unaware what J'Nita was contemplating.. "Many years of the past all bundled together in this room. One day or one week is not sufficient time to finish, she calculated as she hesitated and surveyed the room.

"You know, I can still remember as a child climbing the stairs laboring towards the attic. I couldn't wait to come up here and discover another world. Invariably, I would look out of the window and see small wonders and discoveries. I have seen those trees as monuments and natural wonders,"…

"Mama," interrupted J'Nita. Amalya hesitated to notice her daughter. "What is it," she asked.

"I was wondering … I know we can't explore all of the history of our family today, but is it possible to make one last inquiry.

"About what," questioned Mrs. Harmon.

"About Grandpa Jacque," replied J'Nita.

"We're back from that now; we're standing here and touching each other and talking and what that means is the past is gone. It was nearly impossible the first time and I don't see how we can accomplish that again. We have to be grateful for what we discovered," explain Amalya.

"Oh, I am," said J'Nita defensively, "but I was wondering if Grandpa Jacque's brothers ever followed him north and whether they ever heard from the other siblings who left before emancipation."

"Well now, you're posing some intriguing questions and causing me to recall a little something about what was related a long time ago. As a matter of fact, the return of the other siblings was quite an occasion. It's family lore and now you will hear how it happened." ...

"It was like a family reunion the day all of the Thornton's came together. It was exceptional because the undeniable fact was apparent to everyone that Mama's wishes and prayers had been answered. There was more joy among the Thornton's than ever. Even Grandpa Jacque who everyone thought would never return south, joined the siblings. It was said when he saw everyone together, he announced: 'Time nor circumstance could not keep us apart; we have come full circle.' "That's what I recall, and that's just the surface because we don't have time to delve too deeply," explained Amalya with a sense of high elation about what they had experienced.

J'Nita noticed her mother's demeanor that appears when a person is transformed   from one mind to the other.   J'Nita shared at least part of what had taken place, and was of the mind that they could go back and learn the one last thing she yearned to know. She now had more courage to prod her mother about the Thornton family history.

Amalya had returned to the task of sorting things and was scrutinizing and deciding what to do with each item. What overshadowed her task were thoughts of Grandma and the impossible experience into the past that changed their lives. At the moment, it was like Grandma was the guiding spirit ordering and describing what had taken place and what should be done.

J'Nita approached her mother, realizing that she should not hesitate another second without asking her mother what she fervently yearned:

"Can we travel back to that time again?" J'Nita asked pleadingly. She waited impatiently for her mother's reply, and hoped she would say it was possible.

Startled by the question, Amalya considered an explanation. The experience still held its influence upon both of them and the present seemed far removed because they had not settled or resolved what had taken place. Amalya set aside what she was doing and stood next to J'Nita. She placed her arm around her and guided her towards the window where they perceived the past awaited them. They resolved there was a way to connect the past once again and see their ancestors gathered together as Grandma had described. The glare from the sun seemed to reflect the image of that day. Both peered through the window catching sight of the tree that cast a large shadow and the past appeared before them.

.

Chapter 10

Sibling Rivalry

The tree changed in view, became taller and wider like a century's growth that yields stature and eminence. The land extended beyond the horizon expanding far and wide and becoming a place. Grandma's yard disappeared and in its place was an immense tract of land where people stood or meandered and houses were situated throughout. Amalya and J'Nita followed the land, the people and houses until they found what they believed to be the homestead of the Thornton's. They were assured it was the residence of the Thornton's when they caught a glimpse of Emily and Leona. The two of them seemed to be peering across the land like they were searching for someone or something. Amalya and J'Nita felt they were standing face to face with them and ready to pursue an acquaintance, but were reminded once again that if they made one utter the impossible journey into the past would end.

Amalya and J'Nita watched their ancestors' *every move. They perceived the vast changes in the land* *and surroundings. Time made an indelible impression* *on them. Their experiences were etched in the annals* *of time to be remembered infinitely. Their eyes circled* *the entire tract of land, absorbing every detail with* *interest and curious anticipation. ...*

The modest homestead was well attended. The porch was the length of the house. Shutters were around the windows and the white light made it appear brighter as prisms of colors reflected in bright rays of sun.   A picket fence fortressed a garden within covered with flowers and shrubbery that Emily and Leona had planted. They frequently surveyed the grounds and tended to anything out of place.   Early morning found Emily and Leona ordering the landscape and gardens. They were solitary in their task and hardly a word was exchanged between them.

Afterwards, they would look afield as if still adjusting to how their lives had transformed and the others who had remained on the homestead. Many of the former slaves had become sharecroppers like their brothers Samuel and Elijah. Every morning Samuel and Elijah were on the field before daybreak and worked until dusk. They had families now and the imperative that had once been about leaving the plantation was no longer discussed since emancipation became law. They had seen a great migration from the plantation; slaves who couldn't wait to see how the conflict was going to be settled, set out on the long road to freedom and an uncertain destiny like Jacque.

Each day, Emily and Leona wondered why Samuel and Elijah had not followed Jacque north like they thought they would. They thought Samuel and Elijah would change their minds about sharecropping and take to the road like many others. Often they were in trepidation about whether their departure would ever happen. When they saw them on the field in the morning, it was another day of great relief.

"I don't know what we would have done if Samuel and Elijah went north," admitted Leona.

"I'm afraid to think about it because it can still happen," reminded Emily.

"Now you talking; it's a feeling I have all the time." There's been plenty comings and goings around this place. We've got to expect just about anything," Leona reasoned.

"Slaves free to leave or stay according to the law. Those who come here from other places expect to stay here for some time. It's like Jacque, he had his notions about the north and we couldn't convince him otherwise. I wonder about him from time to time, and if he will ever return here" admitted Emily as she peered in the distance.

"I believe Jacque be returning soon. I heard Papa's creaking wagon as far way as it vanished the day Jacque and his family left," explained Leona.

"It's only natural for you to think that. We didn't take kindly to Jacque leaving anyway, but he was free to do so. He writes us from time to time to let us know he's alive and well. Who knows what will happen. Dreams are things hoped for. We have to believe that one day he will return."

They silently relished the thought with a sense of hope as they watched groups of people on the field work in continuity. Everything appeared natural and the same as they had always observed except they were distracted by a procession of people traveling in a wagon and walking towards them. They stared with alarm at each other and wondered what to anticipate.

"They farmers," wondered Emily upon seeing them.

"I don't know," said Leona doubtfully.

"Maybe Samuel or Elijah sent them here," reasoned Emily as she continued to watch them approach.

"We find out soon. I declare, I was expecting people today," insisted Leona.

"I know what you're thinking, but don't get your hopes up," advised Emily.

"It could be Jacque as well as anybody else, but I'm not fixing to be disappointed," commented Leona.

"That don't appear to be Jacque; too many people," Emily observed.

"Jacque told us he has three children now," Leona reminded her.

"All the people I see aren't children," said Emily as she continued to stare at the approaching wagon of people.

"They just about at our doorstep, how we presenting ourselves," Leona questioned.

Emily made a quick scrutiny and then decided: "I'm like this every day except Sunday and this isn't Sunday. I wasn't expecting a soul."

"We certainly weren't. I guess it don't matter if we're just plain folk on an ordinary day," added Leona as she straightened her clothing and patted her hair to make certain it was in place.

"They're stopping their wagon," announced Emily with rising anxiety.

"I can see it's not Jacque. They're strangers," Leona noted.

"We've greeted strangers before and sent them on their way. They're probably lost," Emily surmised. "We listen carefully to find out."

Both of them exerted effort to appear calm, as they watched a couple of the strangers step down from the wagon and walk in their direction. As they drew nearer, they could see they were men walking wearily. Soon they were faced to face peering at each other awkwardly. The men, fraught with decorum and manners, removed their hats and then greeted them: "Afternoon, Mam," they began. "We haven't been around here for quite some time and were wondering if we travel to the place where the Thornton's live."

Emily and Leona were immediately disarmed when they heard their name spoken by the strangers. They had expected another kind of inquiry, maybe directions or other names, any name but Thornton. They did not know what to say or how to react. Emily pulled Leona aside and whispered: "They know something about us."

"I hear it," commented Leona suspiciously. Feeling the scrutiny of the strangers upon them, they decided to give a reply to the inquiry. "There's more than one Thornton around here," they informed.

"I guess that's true," reasoned the man as he pursued his inquiry. "It's hard because we're not exactly strangers, but it's been some years and a lot of changes.

"It isn't unusual to be lost around here the way things have been lately," interrupted Leona. "We might be able to direct you if you give us the right name."

"Yes, I understand," commented the man as he sought to clarify the matter. "We're inquiring about Viola Thornton in particular," he finally divulged.

Once the words were pronounced, comprehension arose slowly between Emily and Leona. How could they begin to believe that the strangers had anything to do with their mother. So incredible was it to them that they were certain it was a misunderstanding. They were now more wary and in pursuit of a motive.

"'Viola Thornton," reiterated Emily

"You say Viola Thornton," Leona echoed.

"It's been a number of years; too many since we last seen Viola Thornton," the strangers continued.

Emily and Leona stared at them not knowing what to say or what to do. Some thoughts became apparent, but still they were suspicious and afraid to surmise beyond a mere coincidence. Their silent probing persisted and aroused their concern.

"You certain about the name "Thornton," Emily questioned again.

"It's been a number of years since we've seen Viola Thornton, but we certain this is the place and we would be grateful if you could direct us where she live," insisted the strangers.

"That's difficult, commented Leona somberly.

"That's very difficult," added Emily.

"She's not living," questioned the men.

"It's been some years now," Emily replied.

Emily and Leona noticed a sense of regret displayed by the men which caused them to wonder.

"Why are you asking about Viola Thornton?"

They quietly bowed their heads in contemplation and appeared forlorn. What had occurred many years ago now haunted them. It was hopeless to believe that they would see Viola Thornton, but they held on to the last possibility believing that if they told them who they were, they would give them directions to where she might be.

"We her relatives; we her sons and that's her daughter back there waiting to hear."

Emily and Leona were appalled by the stranger's pronouncement. They gazed at the men like staring at ghosts. They nearly fainted as their minds became disoriented. Since they could remember, their siblings' disappearance was a long held mystery that disturbed their mother greatly. The stories about them were legend and many surmises were discussed about what happened to them. All of them had resigned to the fact that they would never see them again. Now time had made the past and its memories a mere second. All of the years of uncertainty and worry changed in a flash. It took Emily and Leona a while to realize the magnitude of what was revealed to them. They stood in a well of disbelief. Deep down they wanted what they heard to be true, but how could it be? Everything was lost in time. They couldn't remember what their siblings looked like. Presently they appeared to be travelers in search of direction. Were they really Thornton's, they began to wonder.

"I know we're not imagining," Leona managed to comment faintly. I must touch you to know I'm not imagining." Both of them were weary with impossibility and what was before them. They felt compelled to lash out to make certain what they heard and what they saw was real. If only their mother were alive, she would certainly recognize her children and they would not have to cast doubt. for they were too young to remember their siblings. They searched for reassurance.

"They say they are our family," Leona commented in a whisper.

"That's what we heard," Emily assured her as they held each other like anchors. The mystery of the past had sent tremors through them. "I think we must find out if they are our siblings for sure," Emily decided.

"They're still standing there; I believe it's real," commented Leona. "Lord, the power of faith all these years."

"I think they resemble the Thornton's when you look at them closely," Emily observed. I often wondered about the possibilities all these years; we were hoping this would happen but never knowing if it ever would. With all the changes we've seen, I think this is the day for the Thornton's."

"If we don't say something, they are going to begin to wonder," prompted Leona.

"You must understand, we wouldn't know. We heard about siblings run away from here; if you be the ones, Mama's at peace today. You see, Viola Thornton you looking for is our Mama and she's not here any more."

The men fell silent when they were finally told about Viola Thornton, their mother. The truth was before them like the night they hid behind the cabin and waited until they thought it was safe to run for freedom. The hope of their dreams was real and tangible and they yearned for nothing more than freedom. The night held their promise and they did not look back. Now they were confronted with a loss they never believed would happen. Mama was always there, reminding them and cautioning them. The thought of never seeing their mother again compounded their grief and they exerted every fiber of their will not to display their regret and the compelling urge to cry out.

Transformed by the men's appearance, Leona and Emily were wondering and beginning to notice them more closely. They were like Jacque, Samuel and Elijah, they decided, but they were afraid to make the final determination. They needed Samuel and Elijah to see them and hear them also. They were more driven by the truth that was before them when they heard them announce:

"I'm Henry and that's Ezekiel; Mandolin is over there waiting. We were hoping against time, you understand, that Mama might still be alive. We sorry to hear she's not. We return with the burden of freedom to see our family."

Leona and Emily carefully studied the strangers professing to be their siblings. Every word and action brought them greater understanding and reality of the barriers of time and separation. Knowledge and truth were still hedging within them. They wanted to embrace their siblings and be accepting but were still reluctant. They continued to listen to the strangers explain.

"When emancipation became law, it occurred to us there was something missing in our lives; something we flee from without thought. We began to wonder about Mama and were hoping to find her here. We sad to hear she isn't here anymore. Where is she buried on this land," the strangers wanted to know.

As they waited for Emily and Leona to reply, they peered at the homestead and throughout the plantation. Memories of the life they once lived were vague and they could not say for certain if the house they peered at was the same place they were born. It looked different and new. What readily obscured any other memories was the dark night when they fled the plantation and became free citizens. They thought their actions were just; if only their siblings knew how they tried to return to free them also, they would understand their dilemma. Being free did not allow them to readily return to slavery for any reason. They had spent many years reliving the moment of their escape and each time they believed they had acted according to the laws of human nature and the will to be free. When they became mature enough to realize and to understand the fullest intent and meaning of the ideals upon which they based their actions, they felt exonerated, but hopeless about their mother and siblings. When they touched the land of freedom, they were different citizens able to walk and talk freely and do things they had never dreamed.

Often they would think about their mother from self-loathing and guilt. When emancipation was proclaimed, they knew the moment had arrived for them to return. Now the past and present had converged rendering them a sense of condemnation when they learned their mother had deceased. They waited precariously not knowing whether their siblings would recognize and accept them as their mother readily would have.

Emily and Leona could not decide entirely and completely. They had acknowledged some things; the evidence of their story was reason to believe that there was a connection; that they might be Thornton's, but they needed Samuel and Elijah also.

"This is more than we bargained for today. I see a resemblance and who else would know about Viola Thornton, our Mama," commented Leona.

"But you still skeptical," Emily questioned.

"That's not entirely the reason. We have to get word to Samuel and Elijah," said Leona, looking in their direction and gathering the details that were still alien to her and realizing when she divulged what had taken place, it might sound too incredible for them to consider. "I have to go and start the goading; it's going to take a lot to convince them what has happened today. I can't say for sure, but I believe they can help."

"You got ample proof; you shouldn't be too long, prompted Emily.

Leona headed for the field thinking and feeling exhilarated. She thought of the words to describe to them what had taken place and imagined their reaction. She saw them staring in disbelief like she still was and not quite certain about the truth. The strangers who walked across the field and confronted them loomed predominately and she could only wonder if they were

Thornton's. Her mother's last words came back to remind her; it was the other sad thing that she would never see. Well, she thought, today she would be happy for if those strangers were really Thornton's, her mother is at peace. The gentle breeze of consciousness made her heart ache and her mind go limp by the memory. The sun seemed intolerably scorching and pervasive and she suddenly stopped. Samuel and Elijah were just a few feet away. They noticed her approach and took the opportunity to rest briefly.

"It's not evening yet; did we miss something," they wanted to know.

Leona noticed they were both impatient as they leaned on the plow waiting to hear what she had to explain. She gathered herself as she thought about the strangers still back at the homestead claiming to be Thornton's and what Samuel and Elijah might find incredible to comprehend once she tells them the reason for her appearance.

"You won't believe this, uh …" Leona began in hesitation.

"Say your peace before the day ends. What is it," they insisted.

Nearly breathless, Leona continued: "Visitors appeared at the door not long ago, and not just any strangers looking for directions … uh … she paused still finding it difficult to relate to them what had taken place.

"Go on, who are they," Elijah insisted.

"Well, you know what Mama wished to happen to the family?"

Both of them reflected briefly but were too impatient to consider the question. "What is it," Samuel asked anxiously.

"I'll give you the benefit of the doubt out here laboring," Leona commented as she began to explain. "Mama always hoped that one day all her children would be together."

"That's right," said Elijah remembering suddenly, "but Mama died before that happened."

"Well, sometimes yearning and wishes are stronger than we can ever imagine; they can carry moments into decades and centuries and even beyond the grave. We had given up ever seeing our siblings, but as fate would have it, I declare," Leona exclaimed as she clasped her hands and peered skyward as if what had occurred was still implausible, "what I'm trying to tell you is going to sound like something out of a dream, but today, ... her words were stifled and difficult for her to utter as the reality became apparent ... Emily and I looked up and who should we see but Ezekiel, Henry and Mandolin."

After Leona made the announcement to Samuel and Elijah, she remained in awe thinking about what had taken place and how impossible it seemed, but her brothers were not convinced. In fact, they reacted with indignation.

"Let's finish what we were doing because Leona came all the way her to interrupt us with dream and imagination. Interruptions don't help us finish what we're doing," admonished Elijah.

Leona, however, was certain of what she knew and what she believed to be true: The Thornton siblings who had been missing all those years had returned and were waiting at the homestead.

"I know it sounds incredible, but it's true as surely as I stand here. If you look in the direction of the house, you will see a host of people standing and waiting, and they are the siblings who run away years ago," explained Leona.

Both Samuel and Elijah peered in the direction Leona guided them, but only a blur covered their eyes from the brightness of the sun.

"We can't see a thing," they both admitted.

"The glare from the sun is blocking your vision," Leona realized. "If you walk towards the house, you'll see a pleasant sight and the truth of what I came to tell you."

"It can wait," Samuel decided impatiently.

"It can't wait. Mama's wish came true today and you have to see for yourself," prompted Leona. If there was a way she could convince them to go immediately and resolve the mystery, she would use it, but they were set in their ways and pulling them away from their work involved a lot of urging. She could hear their muted discussion as they contemplated what they should do.

Both of her brothers looked toward the homestead and perceived that there were people nearby. They observed Leona who was still euphoric and in a state they had not seen before. They conferred privately and decided: "If we intend to continue the day's work, I think we should stop for the time it takes us to get Leona back to the house and see who it is she's talking about."

"It can't be our siblings, maybe some imposters, but I saw people passing through here not long ago. It didn't occur to me to ask who they were and where they were going," said Elijah.

"You say you saw people passing through here," Samuel reiterated.

"Not long ago," replied Elijah.

Samuel became more concerned about who the strangers might be. "I think we should go right away and see who's standing around the homestead

Finally, they beckoned Leona and all of them walked apace towards the homestead.   As they proceeded, both Samuel and Elijah began to wonder if the strangers could be their siblings? Too many years had passed and, unlike Leona and Emily, they never imagined or dreamed they would ever see them again. Nothing could prepare them for what they were about to discover.

As they walked towards the homestead, Leona was of one mind, believing the strangers were their siblings and Samuel and Elijah were of another. They hadn't thought of the siblings in the way their sisters had. They had decided many years ago that freedom was far greater than anything they could hold them liable for. A surge of guilt under the hot sun singed their memory of the many times they thought of running for freedom also. They wiped trickles of moisture as they walked briskly and thought inquisitively as to who the strangers might be. If they were the siblings, how would they receive them, they wondered. A strange emotion overwhelmed them, they had never expected to travel back in the past. Jacque had left under different circumstances and they knew and understood how they would greet him, but the siblings who ran away, there were questions; they had to see them first.

Standing on the porch, Emily's heart raced with anticipation as she watched her brothers and Leona approach.   The mystery of the strangers would be resolved, she thought, for Samuel and Elijah would know if the strangers were their siblings. Inwardly, she wanted them to be their siblings for she wanted to believe that her mother's hope and wishes were far greater than anything imaginable and emancipation made what they were witnessing possible.

When she saw Samuel and Elijah's demeanor, she sensed Leona had probably not done her best convincing. Face to face, she could see that they were agitated and impatient like they were in the midst of a cruel joke. That was the least of their worries, however, as they began to scrutinize the strangers who claimed to be Thornton's. Some of their thoughts and questions became apparent as their memories reverted back to points and time of familiarity. They had to be confident in what they assessed and believed to be true. It was a wide space of events between then and now, but Samuel recollected his part and Elijah did the same. There were things both of them remembered and held onto without realizing they would be called upon for the moment they presently encountered. The mystery of their siblings' disappearance haunted them until time made it a dream to be forgotten. They looked beyond half expecting their mother to appear suddenly and help them solve the mystery before them. When that did not occur, they looked at each other for decision. They probed and provoked to detect a misunderstanding or mockery for they knew emancipation was creating strange situations and circumstances and they were not willing to readily accept the strangers' explanation. Their weather-hued skin possessed knowledge and maturity as they considered what was before them. Working under the scorching sun was one thing, but what was before them was entirely another. The season would produce harvest and they could look out across the land and be assured But with the situation before them, there were no real assurances, Samuel and Elijah realized as they scrutinized the strangers, only high probability and wonder; the years had taken there toll; the strangers claiming to be Thornton's could be anyone. The image and recognition of their siblings was like a dark void. They had nothing to compare. They felt awkward in their scrutiny and felt conscious of their stares. Their minds were moving and rippling like water; they wanted to understand and know the truth about the strangers. Some uncanny thoughts began to arise: maybe they were distant relatives. Suddenly, Elijah pulled Samuel aside: "I'm thinking at this moment what Mama reminded us about."

"I remember," said Samuel as if they had one mind to solve the conflict. "Those siblings are like branches."

"Yes, yes," agreed Elijah "and if we should see them, remember that," added Elijah.

"I suspects we might be looking at those falling branches," Samuel began to realize. "Many years have passed and I'm wondering how we look at strangers and say they siblings."

"It's difficult for sure," admitted Elijah.

"Where we start," Samuel questioned.

"We start by telling Emily and Leona we believe those strangers could be our siblings, but we must act with caution," Elijah suggested.

"All these people coming and going throughout the plantation, it never occurred to me that some of them might be our siblings. I had forgotten about them," commented Samuel.

"All of us had," Elijah added

"I guess we make up our minds to see about those strangers," said Samuel prompting Elijah. Together they walked towards Emily and Leona to discuss what they should do.

Samuel and Elijah could sense the tension between their sisters and the strangers. Their sisters looked anxious and the strangers had a look of hopelessness and sorrow which caused them to take note; they weren't quite sure what to make of it, as they turned to their sisters to beckon them away from audible distance of the strangers.

"Y'all decide about the strangers," they wanted to know immediately.

"They tell you their names," asked Elijah.

"They give the names Mama told us years ago. What other Thornton's you know with those names but Mama's children," replied Leona.

"That can't be a coincidence. Besides, when you search their faces, there's something that tells you they are Thornton's. You have to consider this is the result of emancipation. They can't be slaves again and maybe that's why they return because freedom is the law now," Emily surmised.

The Thornton's who had never left the plantation a day in their lives, had been slaves and free citizens in the same place did not know the faces of other Thornton's, but they had to decide about the strangers claiming to be Thornton's who had returned from the past and created a dilemma for them. The truth was harder to accept after so many years and not as much as a word to know if they were dead or alive. They wanted to believe they were Thornton's and they wanted to abide by their mother's advice, but there was conflict. Even though birthright and history had given the other siblings the right to their family and generations, laws of nature and laws of the land can be in opposition.

Samuel, followed by the others, confronted the men claiming to be Thornton's. It was natural for him to give a longer stare for doubt still remained. "What name Thornton's are you," he asked.

"I'm Ezekiel Thornton," one of strangers replied immediately. "I always went by that name."

"I'm Henry Thornton. I keep the same name. We wanted to be known as the Thornton's who were free. That's Mandolin and our families over there," he said looking in the direction of the group of people waiting.

"The new law give us hope and we came back to see Mama, but that's our lost and sorrow," commented Ezekiel somberly.

"The years in freedom give us determination. At the time, it seemed the only thing to do. Freedom was ours to keep; we tried to return many times to free our family, but we were cautioned and even threatened to be returned and we didn't want that to happen. We lived in hope that one day we would see our family again.

Samuel turned to his siblings to confer with them privately: "It's been a lot of years, and Mama did a lot of praying and her last words were about the siblings that run away. If the truth is before us, we'll see the Thornton come from them naturally. It 's a matter of time, but we can't turn them away and say they impostors," he persuaded the others. All of them dismissed their fears and doubts about the strangers and accepted them like relatives who had come to visit them from faraway.

"A family coming together at this time can only mean good days ahead. There's been a lot of comings and goings when emancipation became law, you understand, and we can't be too careful about whose moving across the land. We've been here all our lives. We hear about you and knew it was a dangerous undertaking at the time, but for a life of freedom, who could judge. Freedom is every person's desire. We can't deny you are the siblings Mama told us about. Mama had faith that one day we would be together and I guess this is the day chosen."

Samuel beckoned Emily, Leona and Elijah towards him for it was the moment they decided to join together and accept the strangers as siblings. They appeared liberated as they embraced them in acknowledgement of what they determined. All of them looked in the direction of Mandolin and called her to join them. Especially Emily and Leona were in high anticipation about who Mandolin might resemble. When she approached and became more visible they were immediately astonished by the Thornton similarities and were more certain that the strangers were Thornton's.

"Mama is resting in peace for sure," commented Leona.

"Our Mama buried somewhere on this land," Henry asked anxiously.

Emily and the others became silent as the question loomed like a burden placed upon them. They reacted mysteriously for they remembered their mother's last words and a sense of guilt had arisen. It was not that they did not want to reveal their mother's resting place, but an unknown barrier prevented them.

"I guess it's natural to want to know where Mama's buried. It's our duty, as Thornton's to show you around this place, and maybe before long, we'll show you Mama's resting place. It's not easy, you understand, at this time," explained Samuel.

"We will be grateful to see the Thornton plantation. Our memories have failed us after all these years.   If I'm not mistaken, I believe this cabin changed," Henry noted.

Both Leona and Emily nodded to confirm what he had observed. Freedom bring change. This house is now our homestead. We didn't see fit to leave here when Master Thornton give us our freedom," commented Emily.

"I believe we should show them around the place now," interrupted Samuel. He beckoned Elijah and both of them gathered the siblings and their families and escorted them in the direction of the field. Emily and Leona watched them walk across the earth and did not cease their vigilance until they saw them vanish into a corridor of the land their eyes could not follow.

Emily and Leona remained on the porch looking afar in amazement wondering if they were in dream and never wanting to turn away. They watched the near perfect day in the fullness of spring and a liveliness they had not seen since they were given their freedom. They were nearly afraid to marvel or conjecture; their emotions were tangled in an uncertain joy. They didn't know what broke the trance maybe silhouettes flitting back and forth like illusions, but they found themselves in the parlor of the house deciding what bearing the appearance of their siblings would have on their lives.

They were still single women courting with ideas of marriage and family. All along it was what had transpired – the return of the siblings – that had delayed their decisions. It was like the natural order of things proceeding: an occurrence had to take place before another. Deep within, they knew it would not be much longer.   Mama's wish had come to bear and posthumous happenings are a reminder to those witnessing of the possibilities. They imagined themselves like Mandolin whom they had only seen briefly but right away the connection formed like blood in the veins. One day all of them would look at this day and their families and reminisce like it was happening all over again; but there was at least one other matter they needed to attend. Emily and Leona looked at each other when the thought occurred. Neither could resist informing the other: "We must get word to Jacque right away," they uttered simultaneously.

"Has it occurred to you," questioned Leona.

"What," said Emily as she searched for pencil and paper.

"We might see Jacque and his family any day now. I'm sure when he hears that the siblings have returned, he will travel south, Leona commented.

"I know, he will be wondering a long time what the words mean," surmised Emily.

"It will be hard for him to comprehend being so far away, but he'll realize what Mama always hoped," reminded Leona.

"We'll send word right away," urged Emily.

Chapter 11

The South Beckons

The Antislavery Society was still the haven and outpost many slaves discovered when they arrived in the city. The Society depended on Jacque for his continued commitment, and most evenings found him exhorting the newly freed slaves of the ways and wiles of the city, for the Society had many incidents were slaves were imprisoned or returned to the south. Jacque helped a multitude of slaves settle and adjust to northern life. On each occasion, it never ceased to remind him of his experiences when he arrived in the city. He did everything within his power to make life an easier transition for the newly arrived slaves, for being under the hover of the sun was different than being surrounded by mortar, brick, distant heights and many other things the newly freed slaves had never seen before. When Jacque noticed a waver of will in any of them, he would invariably remind them: "In time, the north will mean promise." Once he had instilled a sense of caution and direction in the newly arrived slaves, he watched them leave filled with more certainty about their prospects and living in the city.

Thereafter, he would return home in the evening reveling in thoughts of his experiences when he arrived in the city. He especially thought of the docks and the harbor and imagined the different places the newly arrived slaves had traveled. The notion of freedom was entertained in every possible way until he confronted his family.

He was always reassured when he found his family safe. Jacque and Willa now had three children: Jacque, Jr., Marian and Viola, the oldest. Always, when observing his children, he thought how time and history had transformed their lives. The law of the land made them free and before that his freedom made them free. They would never wonder about whether they were slaves like he had done when he was their age or dream of freedom. His children were free. They only had to dream and maybe their small visions would become their greatest expectations.

As they engaged in play, he ruminated about the turn of events, and how proslavery proponents were still resisting. The Society had anticipated the remaining conflict and was doing everything within its power to help resolve the conflict. Sometimes when Jacque became apprehensive about the perils of the ending war, he would breakaway from his thoughts and lift the children high above their stance and listen to them shrill and giggle and know for that moment there was a sense of peace. He hoped he could tell his children for the rest of their lives they were free. When it appeared they had become weary, Willa was nearby ready to settle the children for the evening.

On this particular evening, Willa was unusually anxious and made her concerns known to Jacque.

"I'm glad this day is over. All day I worried about this letter we received from down home," she divulged as she handed the letter to Jacque.

"There's no need to worry, we've received word from Emily and Leona before," commented Jacque as he scrutinized the envelope.

Willa watched him inspect the envelope carefully and even though he voiced little concern about the letter, she detected his caution.

"I'll open it to find out what they're informing us about his time," Jacque commented.

Willa drew closer to Jacque as he unfolded the letter and began to read silently. Gradually he became immersed in the contents of the letter. Willa waited anxiously to hear what new developments had taken place down home. With emancipation, many regions were transforming, but the southern region was resisting the new law. She imagined many terrible things even as she hoped that no one was hurt or dead or something worse that was beyond her comprehension. She wanted Jacque to allay her fears immediately.

Soon she noticed his changed manner and still wasn't sure what to make of the situation. Jacque stared distantly and was momentarily speechless. She had to urge him for explanation.

"What they telling us," she asked.

"I can't believe what they say. Here, you read this letter," he offered, "because it doesn't seem right."

Willa took the letter and began to read, but her patience was expended and she could barely comprehend the words. When she finished, she stared at Jacque with more perplexity than ever about the contents of the letter.

"I don't know, Jacque, they're writing about something I never heard before," Willa commented as she returned the letter to Jacque.

"We're many miles away and it's hard to understand the meaning of everything. There's much to consider in this time of change. They're writing us about the siblings who disappeared and who we never expected to see again," said Jacque in a raspy barely audible voice.

"I don't know your other siblings," admitted Willa, "but I guess they wanted you to know about their return."

"I don't know how I feel; I don't know what to think." admitted Jacque vacantly. "All those years not knowing if our siblings were dead or alive, it's hard to imagine it's real." Jacque hesitated in thought as he recollected the day he left the homestead. He was placed in the midst of the vast land and what had taken place many years ago. Memories of his past appeared vividly in his mind as if he were actually back home.

"I'm wishing now what I thought I'd never say," Jacque hesitated as he thought about the hard fought battle he waged to be a free man and to be where he was presently. "Sometimes life turns you around and makes you look at it in another way."

"It must be hard to believe that your siblings returned. It's a good thing they wrote to let us know, so you won't feel like a stranger to the place you were born," commented Willa.

"It's about many things. I was thinking … it was a long time ago, but hearing about our siblings makes it feel like yesterday. Mama had a lot of faith and I guess she allowed us some too. She never once believed our siblings were dead. I should have known one day we would hear from them, it was just a matter of time. We must consider making a trip down home," Jacque finally decided.

"I never thought I'd hear you talk about returning home," admitted Willa.

"Emancipation has brought change, and freed slaves are traveling all over this land. Mama always wanted us to be together and if you've never seen our other siblings, you're about to see all of the Thornton's alive and well as Mama had hoped. We leave as soon as we can," said Jacque decisively."

Chapter 12

Mandolin's Tale

Emily and Leona were in awe about what was occurring. Each morning they awakened to see their modest dwelling now a thoroughfare with people coming and going and offering to help. They were in high anticipation as the reunion neared. Everything seemed so incredible, they thought they were dreaming until they saw their siblings who had returned and they knew it was reality. It wasn't going to be an ordinary reunion, but a day to remember for a lifetime. Emily and Leona involved themselves in every detail of the preparations and made certain everything was handled with the utmost consideration.

One morning, they were outwitted when they opened the door to find Mandolin standing bright-eyed and eager to help in anyway she could.

"Something tells me another pair of hands will help the occasion," she commented as they invited her in. Her first appearance was the most awkward because of the difficulty they had making room for a sibling they had forgotten or thought was dead. The adjustments came gradually. Emily and Leona did all they could to make Mandolin feel at home, and they did all they could not to stare and make comparisons. Initially, they thought Mandolin resembled their mother; that was their first impression. But, within a few minutes of her presence, Emily thought she favored Leona and Leona thought she favored Emily. There was a constant change of opinion, but both were finally convinced Mandolin was their sister, and that accepted fact eventually put them at ease.

They had examined Mandolin's round face with features that stood out like a statue. Her hair was tied back and twisted in a bun. Her eyebrows were heavily arched around her searching eyes and oval face. Her warm smile reminded them of their mother and made it easier for them to become acquainted. Mandolin was the oldest by as much as ten years, but she belied her seniority. All of them appeared to be around the same age, but only Mandolin had children: twin boys and a girl. Her children stood like a triangle, the twins side by side and the girl in back of them hidden by the boys' height and size.

When Emily and the others learned they had twin relatives, they were amazed. "How could that be," they questioned. They had never seen twins before. They observed the boys like curiosities at first and saw they had the same resemblance.

"Meet Isaac and Harold," Mandolin said introducing them to her siblings. By now she was used to the reaction by everyone who learned her boys were twins. Then she introduced her daughter, Viola.

"Viola is a favorite name in the family," commented Emily and Leona. "You must be the second one, but soon you'll meet another Viola," both of them added. They realized that it was not a coincidence that the little girl had the same name as their mother, which further diminished any doubt about Mandolin's and their brothers' identity.

Each time Mandolin joined them to help with the preparation, their acquaintance became closer as she recollected to Emily and Leona definitive facts about the family. Henry was the oldest and named after the father, followed by Ezekiel, John, Emily, Samuel, Elijah and Leona. Now Emily and Leona were more certain who was the oldest and youngest. The older children remember their father, but his sudden death prevented any close relationship. "Henry can tell you more about our father than any of us," Mandolin related. Many issues and circumstances about the past were detailed by Mandolin. One story in particular held Emily and Leona enthralled. Every preparation ceased as they listened to Mandolin detail how they escaped to freedom.

They sat at the kitchen table where they usually would and provided a chair for Mandolin who placed it in the center so that Leona was on one side and Emily on the other. Emily and Leona waited anxiously to hear about the sibling's mysterious disappearance that sent the Thornton plantation in turmoil and caused their family to be the object of suspicion, not to mention the sadness their mother experienced.

The years did little to abate the memories Mandolin had about the escape. Her voice sounded like rust that had to be cleared away to get to the smooth surface. All of them realized that words had never been formed about the incident. Mandolin began the story with uneven, disconnected words at first.

"We ... I ... they ... sometimes ... we didn't want to ... but freedom kept us wanting and thinking about escape." Mandolin sounded like a frightened child telling an awful and terrifying secret as her calm composure began to fray. She twisted her hands unconsciously like confusion made words difficult to utter. Her face became moist and her appearance worried.

"It was a long time before we actually made a run for it. Many days and not so much as a word was exchanged between us about our plan to escape. We had to get courage and we had to be certain because if we weren't certain, we could be caught and that's the last thing we wanted to happen. I wasn't certain. I wasn't certain when I first learned about it and I wasn't certain the night we ran for freedom. Henry learned about runaways and how they had reached freedom without getting caught and that gave him the notion to try. He learned also that there were people who helped runaways because they didn't think slavery was just."

...

"One day, I saw Henry and Ezekiel gathered too close to measure and it struck me that something very important was being discussed between them. The longer I stood, the longer they remained talking. When I approached them, words occurred to me like: "You must be talking about freedom because wouldn't nothing else cause you to act so mysterious. They startled in surprise at first, but when they saw it was me, they said, without hesitation: 'Yes, we're talking about freedom.' When the words were said and they realized what they had admitted, they began to worry. They looked at me with narrowed, fearful eyes. 'Freedom is every man's dream. Nothing should stop a man from freedom.' All of us became silent, because we knew we were talking wild dreams and if anyone had the slightest idea what we intended, something awful would happen, and that was our greatest fear, what terrible thing could happen to us for what we were thinking and what we were discussing. We thought of all the punishments we had heard about; the lashings, separations and scorn and were horrified, but we still wanted our freedom. When you hear about freedom and know there are ways to gain it, the dream is real."

"That day changed our lives. We became one in our quest for freedom. It never occurred to us that we would be abandoning the family. We wanted to be known as the Thornton's who were free. That gave us the courage and we didn't think about anything else. Waiting and watching for when we could escape, became an endless vigil, we had to be wary and plan things in a certain way so that when the day arrived, it would be just right.

Many nights I lay in the dark listening and listening in the still quiet of the night; it was a dark silence worse than death; it was like I was waiting for doom. I would inevitably fall asleep. It was never a good sleep from the time I learned about the escape and then waiting for the moment to escape, I didn't sleep well. Dreams and nightmares came more often. Everything was terrifying. I was in a dark field wondering where Henry and Ezekiel were. Sometimes I was running from being chased, knowing if I got caught, I would die or someone would kill me. I ran swiftly; I never knew I could run so fast. When I felt that I couldn't run any longer, my legs began to buckle and ache and I became frightened. I would then awaken fearful, and wonder if Henry and Ezekiel had left for freedom without me. I suffered through that thought until I went to the field. When I finally saw them, I was relieved because I didn't want that dream to be true.

The nightmares and dreams kept appearing; it was nothing I could do about them for as long as it took us to escape. The night before our escape was the worse. It began to bother me about Mama. We were planning to escape and we wouldn't see her anymore. How would that be? Death took Papa and we eventually understood and accepted that, but we were escaping never to return or see the family again. That thought was very hard on us because it wasn't like death, we were running away. I thought through my feelings many nights and couldn't come to terms. I kept evading what I actually felt because when I thought about freedom, I was happy and I didn't want to stop thinking about it. One night I dreamed of freedom. The dark became light; there were people, friendly and accepting us like kin. We walked free and slept free and soon we worked for wages. There were many of us and no matter what happened, we were free. I will never forget the feeling of freedom. I thought the feeling of being free would never leave, but suddenly it grew dark like it was before. I was still in dream but wandering; for a long time I was wandering until I heard a voice call out, then I startled. At first it was faint but gradually grew louder and louder. The louder it grew the more familiar it sounded. I realized for certain it was Mama's voice calling: Mandolin! … Mandolin! I froze in silence. I didn't answer. She continued to call: Mandolin! … Mandolin! Still I didn't answer. Instead, I began to sink deep down into darkness like I was hiding as she called me. The deeper I descended the more her voice became a faint echo. The echoing began to sound like bells reverberating and clanging noisily. Finally, I couldn't tolerate it any longer. My eyes opened to discover the moon in the dark and quiet night. I covered my ears with my hands.

I felt awful. Why didn't I answer Mama, I questioned myself guiltily. I lay inconsolable and afraid. I worried if Henry and Ezekiel had already run for freedom. When morning appeared, my anxiety didn't leave until I saw them in the field. By their appearance, I knew we would run for freedom that night. The world never looked so beautiful to me. I hadn't seen the horizon before, but I looked and saw a different world and thought: soon I will be free."

"I didn't sleep that night. I was punished with anxiety as I lay fully dressed and prepared to run when Henry and Ezekiel gave the signal. Many thoughts crossed my mind as I waited: fear, failure, abandonment, separation, punishment, even death. I wanted to scream, but the thought of freedom restored my courage and I began to think about how I would be one of the free Thornton's and that kept me hopeful and waiting without sleep. Finally, out of the quiet night, I heard rustling. Ordinarily, I wouldn't pay such sounds any attention, but something told me it was Henry and Ezekiel signaling to run for freedom. Surely, when I got up enough nerve to check, I discovered I wasn't mistaken. We didn't speak words as we followed each other closely. We moved swiftly but furtively and hardly a sound was heard between us. We were frightened, just plain frightened that we would be caught, but the longer we traveled, the more determined we became. Traveling in the dark, cold and dampness was hard on us. We got caught in briar patches, sunk in marshes and animals startled us nearly to death, but we trudged on fearful but determined. We looked at the sky and one minute it was a clear dark blue with stars sparkling like crystals, and the next minute, it disintegrated into a gray white, that's when we realized we had traveled through the night. I was more fearful than Henry and Ezekiel that we were lost, but Henry had an idea where we were supposed to travel and knew our destination."

"When it seemed we had no place to go, that the dawn appearing on the horizon would leave us discovered, we stopped and fell into the trenches, rested; wondered; heard each others heavy and fearful breathing; searched for relief and calm; felt our bones begin to ache. Weariness came over us like a sudden douse of water. The cold chill of the cave we descended was as mysterious as our thoughts about what would happen next. Henry tried to quell our fears, explaining to us that we had to wait, we just had to wait, that's all we could do for the time being. Restless, confused and weary, the agony of not knowing was unbearable. We couldn't raise an alarm, we were gripped with thoughts of doom. Why had we run away, I began to question."

"I drifted to sleep, but it wasn't a restful sleep. A dark fear followed me in dream and I could not escape. I dreamed Henry and Ezekiel were fighting and shouting harsh and angry words at each other. I came between them and they pushed me away like they didn't know me. I began to cry, but it was like they didn't hear me. I cried and cried until I woke in muffled sobs. Soon, I quieted and began to listen. I could hear heavy breathing from Henry and Ezekiel. I listened more carefully. It was raining and that made me realize we were still in the cave; that we were safe and still waiting. It rained all day; a thunderous rain like the earth was about to open and destroy us. Tears trickled down as I thought. ...

"I was a young girl, running freely on the Thornton plantation. I remembered Papa and Mama and, at the time everything seemed fine, until one day I saw a wagon coming up the field. It seemed to move slowly because it carried a lot of people. That wasn't unusual, but as I continued to watch, I noticed the people were all bound together in chains. Terror struck in me. I was so horrified. I turned and ran as fast as I could because something told me there was danger. I found Mama and told her about it. That's when I learned about slavery. I'll never forget that day. I have relived it over and over again. ... That night waiting in the dark and cold cave made that day more real than I could ever have imagined. What if we were chained and taken to some strange place. I was in despair. I could only hope and pray that nothing terrible would happen to us.

"When the thunder stopped and the rain subsided, a silence prevailed momentarily until other sounds intruded. As the sounds became more audible, I became more fearful because the voices were those of strangers and I thought we were in imminent danger and would be captured any second. For the first time, Henry and Ezekiel were roused and I was relieved to see they were alert. Soon I realized it was what we had been waiting for, but still I felt uncertain. Henry and Ezekiel were afoot and ready to receive the approaching people. Finally, we made human contact with people who would help us escape to freedom. We left quietly and with the unspoken wisdom that either freedom was near or we were embarking upon a terrible destination. As it turned out, we were on the path to freedom."

"We joined others who had run for freedom. It was mysterious to find out it was real; that we would be free in a matter of days. We saw each others faces but all of us were strangers to each other. We stopped at the Underground Railroad, a place that had long been in our imagination and yearning. It was a long, dark tunnel, wide enough for a train to ride through. The only difference in the Underground Railroad and the cave we left was the Underground Railroad had lanterns for light, yellow glowing rays of hope and we were less fearful. The people who conducted our escape weren't afraid to talk, which made us more certain we weren't going to be sold, but instead were going to reach freedom. It was dangerous for all three of us to travel together, but it was allowed anyway. We traveled as far as New York." ...

"New York," exclaimed Emily barely able to contain her emotions.

"That's were John went," Leona informed.

"You mean to say, you in the same place and didn't run into each other," questioned Emily.

Mandolin began to wonder if she had ever stood face to face with John and didn't recognize who he was. She pondered the possibility momentarily and then commented: "New York is a big place with many people. It's not like here. There, you can pass people along the street and never say a word or know who the people are."

What Mandolin explained sounded incredible to Emily and Leona, but freedom allowed many things to take place that they couldn't comprehend, their siblings' return being the most incomprehensible. They realized with each passing day, they would understand what fate had done to the Thornton family and they decided it was courageous of their siblings to escape to freedom, they only wished they could have found a way to let them know they were alive and well. Suddenly, all of them stood up and embraced each other with certainty and knowledge that they were siblings.

As the preparations for the reunion resumed, all of them individually and collectively conjectured about what would happen on that day. They especially wondered about whether John would return, as they knew his return would sanction the truth that the strangers were Thornton's. The barrier between time diminished and the strangeness became kinship, as sisters related and connected the past and the present.

Chapter 13

Family Reunion

Jacque did not delay preparations for the journey south. He and his family left early one morning with a sense of anticipation and apprehension about traveling south. He wondered what it would be like as he searched for the road that would lead them safely back home. The plantation was prominent in his mind as he traveled, the landscape he worked during his youth, the cabins and buildings situated throughout; the long winding roads and connecting corridors and his siblings. He knew everything had probably changed especially his siblings. He envisioned how emancipation had transformed everything as it was evident as he proceeded on the journey. He thought about what Emily and Leona had informed him about Samuel and Elijah who were now married with children. The return of the other siblings who had runaway years ago was the impossibility upon which

Jacque thought he would never have to venture or consider. The mystery was still like a void in his mind and yet he knew when he arrived at the homestead he would have to confront and decide.

The great migration was conspicuous with people moving unencumbered from place to place. The familiarity of his journey began to assert in his mind as he gradually recollected some experiences. When he left the Thornton plantation, his personal covenant was met and, at the time that was all that mattered because what he dreamed about all his life was made possible. He departed yearning and hoping for the promise like the people who were now traveling to other parts of the country. In the many years away from the homestead, he had, through determination, embraced a world that gave him purpose for his strivings. He had seen and helped downtrodden men and women mount in strides and settle in the north and live out their promise. The Society had given hundreds of people hope to live out their lives to the fullest potential possible. Whenever Jacque thought of the Society it was as a person once lost in the wilderness and one day suddenly discovering a ray of hope.

He had learned about the great men who risked their lives to move slavery closer to being abolished. Frederick Douglas was uppermost in his mind, recalling how he single-handedly freed himself from slavery and then traveled from place to place espousing the cause to abolish slavery. Often, Jacque thought if it weren't for men like Frederick Douglas, Nat Turner, William Still, who was leader of the Underground Railroad, the plight of the multitudes of slaves would still be uncertain. Jacque had the distinct honor of standing shoulder to shoulder with some of the men and hear them propound the evils of slavery and the common right of freedom for all men. Jacque was convinced that the many meetings and gatherings had helped in some way to end slavery. As he traveled, he thought of the countless times slaves and freed slaves had come to the Society in need of help. The individual pleas and the insurmountable burdens stood in the folds of his memory. Faith, hope and promise commingled, one challenging the other but never abandoning.

For miles, the only thing Jacque heard was the clopping of the wagon and the stories of the great men and women who helped bring slavery to an end; it was like light shining a path to a great destination and he was traveling in freedom witnessing the untold changes in his midst. Some of the spirituals sang at the gatherings hummed in his mind and to his surprise he remembered: *Dark and thorny is the path; Where the pilgrim makes his way; But beyond this vale of sorrow, Lie the fields of endless days.* The plaintive strains of the lyrics helped to ease his concerns and the journey seemed less burdensome on his return south than his journey of years ago when he felt his existence was uncertain. "Times have changed," he uttered aloud, distracting Willa.

"Yes, it has," Willa commented. "Everything is different now; we can travel and not worry. I see things I haven't seen before. I've been wondering what it's like back home. You know I have to see my family. I know they won't be the same, and I'm trying to get used to it. I wonder if they are still there."

"Can't say until we get there," said Jacque.

Willa became silent, knowing it was hopeless to expect that her family remained on the plantation after emancipation and if they had gone other places, she would try to find out where. The family that remained had worked hard on the plantation and sometimes she was spared some of the toil because she was their only daughter. When her family learned about Jacque and marriage and that she would be leaving the plantation because he was given his freedom, they did not hesitate to consent. They   tried to explain to her about separation because of freedom. "Every person should be free, and you are the first in our family. No one should stand in freedom's way."   Thus, Willa understood when she left that she might not see them again. Now she was more preoccupied than ever about her family. The reality of whether she would ever see them again, she did not want to accept. She would do all she could to find them, she decided, but she also knew her determination might lead to disappointment if her family had left the plantation. She repressed her despair and instead envisioned them as she had left them. ...

As evening approached, Jacque and Willa were still wondering about the past. The sun moving towards the horizon streaked the sky with a bright crimson glow. They stopped and rested as day drew to a close. Rest did not come easily for Jacque especially; he continued to wonder about his siblings with perplexity. His mother's advice seemed to haunt him like the dark edge of the horizon that ended the day. In the dark, he could only perceive silhouettes of how they might appear, but he sensed their yearning for freedom which led to their escape. How could he hold it against them, he had the same fervent yearning. Freedom was imagination and dream for most of them, but his siblings had attained it. His mother's pliant cry at the lost of her children led to an intolerable despair. Her desire to see all of her children together had outlasted her existence, but her hope was incomprehensible for very soon it would be realized.

At the moment, Jacque wanted to flee and reach the homestead as quickly as possible, but he noticed Willa was quietly resting and the peaceful breathing of sleep from the children he could not disturb. He resigned to resting in the dark space and listening to every sound in the night and the disturbances that made him wary and impatient. He vowed to meet daylight before dream, but that too was impossible. His thoughts of the Georgia plantation and what it might be like presently lulled him to sleep.

In his dreams, he had arrived at the homestead. All of his siblings were there. Everyone was speaking at once and hardly a word was discernible. Laughter replaced what could not be understood. Jacque laughed because he could not speak. He heard his children's laughter and Willa never sounded as joyous since he had known her; which made his laughter greater. When Emily embraced him, her bosom shook him with laughter and Leona's shrilled laughter tickled his ears. He became more joyous and laughed robustly. Soon he was joined by Samuel and Elijah and together their laughter could be heard in the valley echoing spontaneously. Next appeared the other siblings who began to speak words through the laughter. Their utterances were indistinct at first, but they persisted: "I'm Henry Thornton, I'm Ezekiel Thornton, I'm Mandolin Thornton," they reiterated over and over again in Jacque's presence. They noticed Jacque straining for comprehension about what they were uttering. Gradually, Jacque understood and his voice rose above the others: "There's no laughter for those who disappear in the dark." ...

"John!" he heard Emily exclaim. He awakened. It was dawn. He lay in a daze as the dream held its portent. He rubbed his eyes and stared at the blue-gray sky, not knowing what to think. As his thoughts slowly became more lucid, one thought in particular impelled his sudden action: They were due to arrive at the homestead by early evening. In spite of the skepticism that possessed him, he arose quickly and prompted Willa and the children: "We must leave now."

When they returned to the road, it was like night never occurred. They noticed the rays of sun had absorbed the pale gray sky. All of the troubled thoughts receded from memory. There were unobstructed views and vast tracts of land leading to their destination. They rode freely and felt untroubled about any dangers. The whirring return to their birthplace mingled years of absence and years of living in a new land. They were different people now, but unmistakably aware that the past and the present are inextricably bound. They were destined to go north to live in freedom, something that they had only imagined before they ventured their journey to the north.

The miles sped quickly to the south and drew them closer to the past. Their anticipation was high and they seemed to rest in memory of the birthplace they had nearly forgotten. After several hours of travel, Willa was the first to notice where they were and alerted Jacque to also take notice.

"You remember this place," she asked. Jacque surveyed the surroundings and recalled the time they had stopped in the vicinity on their first journey north. He remembered the plantation and the strangers who offered him to sharecrop. At that time, they had their greatest hopes before them and were held captive by the advent of a new south, but Jacque's dreams were set on the north. They looked afar noticing the plantation was still standing and cabins spread throughout.

"We seem to travel back the same way," commented Jacque. "They been free a long time," he said as he drove pass. They had not cleared a few hundred yards before they heard galloping sounds coming towards them. Jacque slowed the wagon and eventually brought it to a stop to meet the approaching men.

"You heading to the Ellis homestead," they wanted to know. There was little time to think of anything other than the men's inquiry. "No, we're looking for another homestead," replied Jacque. The men did not delay as they nodded an understanding and rode away as quickly as they had appeared.

Jacque continued his journey more hopeful than ever before; he didn't have to worry about patrollers who would return him to the plantation, nor did he have to worry about being seen with his family riding as a free man – he was free.

As their destination neared, they began to feel less estranged about the surroundings. The years away from their birthplace made them inclined to see similarities and make comparisons. What they had anticipated began to appear. There was newness all around and the world was quite different from what they had left. Jacque was more drawn to the place than he was prepared to concede. There was vitality and promise throughout as workers labored in the fields. He wondered who were sharecroppers and who were owners for he realized freedom gave them the choice. It occurred to him that Samuel and Elijah could be among the group of people that came into view and he stared more intently to recognize them. The children sensed that they had arrived at the homestead by their parents' reaction and could not contain their excitement.

"Papa, are all of those people our relatives," Viola wanted to know.

"We're not sure yet, we have to find out," Willa replied instead.

Jacque steered the wagon closer and closer like instinct was guiding him to his former dwelling. He stopped suddenly for he knew when he was in front of the home he had been born. An eerie feeling possessed him followed by thoughts and visions of what had taken place. Noticeably, his mother was missing as he was used to seeing her surrounded by his siblings in front of the cabin. He studied the homestead which extended with a porch covering the length of the house. A fence was erected like a fortress and a pathway led to the front door. Jacque's view of his birthplace vanished; everything had changed.

At first, he was overwhelmed by a great sense of lost. His mother was no longer there; the changes were nothing like he envisioned or anticipated. He began to wonder, like a stranger, what he would next encounter. He stepped down from the wagon and walked towards the homestead. He hesitated at the gate, but soon opened it and walked towards the house.

Emily and Leona had noticed Jacque making strides toward the house. They had been anticipating his arrival and were hoping the man walking up the pathway was Jacque. The wagon was different, however, arousing uncertainty in them as they continued to gaze. Their Papa's wagon that Jacque had left the plantation with wasn't as fancy as the one Jacque returned in. The wagon waiting with Willa and the children was enclosed and they were not able to see anyone but Jacque who was by now at the front door.

"I believe I hear him knocking," commented Emily. "That's Jacque, I know him regardless to the long time we haven't seen him," exclaimed Emily.

"There's no question, I can see that for myself," Leona agreed.

"We been expecting him, but Lord, I never thought we'd see him again."

"Those years and miles come right back to us. Look at him, he's as sturdy and proud as the day he left. Let's walk nearby and give a wave so that he knows it's us," Emily suggested.

It was a late summer afternoon when Jacque finally arrived on the homestead.. The sun sparkled with brightness as if inviting him to a new place and time. Jacque felt it was an auspicious day in the making, one that would be long remembered and cherished with time. He saw his sisters walking towards him and waving. He waved back and wondered if they were his sisters, he wasn't sure, but he reacted with reasonable certainty. They met halfway on the path. All of them became disarmed with soaring emotions. Stifled for words, they merely stared with an enigmatic glare of awe and familiarity. Some primordial force compelled them to a moment when they were children. Each of them had harbored similar thoughts as they stared and marveled at where they were and what had taken place.

"Jacque," is that you," both of his sisters exclaimed so loudly it pierced the silence in the mid-afternoon and disturbed Willa and the children who took notice. From afar, they watched siblings meeting and connecting after a long absence. When Willa saw them embrace in kinship, she realized that they were at home and the mystery of her family started her to wondering and looking beyond where they lived not far from Jacque and his family. She was afraid of her thoughts, afraid that when she ventured home that her family would not be there. The unsettling thoughts about her family provoked Willa like never before because distance no longer provided her refuge; now she would discover what happened to her family.

The restlessness of the children distracted Willa and made her look and discover they were standing and watching their father beckon them towards him. Willa arose quickly and urged the children out of the sedan. The children chattered excitedly as they followed their mother. Willa glanced at them to make certain they looked presentable, as they would be meeting Jacque's family for the first time. She brushed their hair back and commanded them to straighten their clothes. She glanced at them in scrutiny and decided they looked okay.

As Jacque and his sisters awaited Willa and the children, they stood grappling with the various thoughts that came to mind. Neither Emily nor Leona could get over the fact that Jacque was standing in their presence, alive and well and looking very vital. Jacque observed in his sisters how plainly dignified and graceful they appeared. The sun was high above them as if to bear them down, but they did not seem to notice. They stood watching Willa and the children approach. Emily and Leona were more excited than they could contain.

"Words can't describe the moment, that's all there is to it," commented Emily.

Emily and Leona had to readjust their view when they saw Willa and the children up close. Jacque had left with wife and infant, but they were seeing how that had changed.

Jacque cleared his voice before speaking. Many emotions were tied to the moment, and he could not readily bellow as he was accustomed.

When he felt he could be heard clearly, he began: "Emily and Leona, you remember Willa, and these are our children, Viola, Marian and Jacque, Jr.

Emily and Leona were nearly speechless, but they managed to coddle the children and embrace Jacque and Willa.

The girls smiled openly like they recognized acceptance and Jacque, Jr. stared wide-eyed from his father's arms.

"Well, as fate would have it, you travel back home and we know the miles have been numerous and have made you weary. You need to rest, Emily directed them towards to house. There's a lot of people – Thornton's – you must see and meet," said Emily as she guided them to the modest dwelling. She beamed with a pride that she could not get used to, one that she never thought she would have or anticipated and wondered if Leona had the same euphoria. She could not help but think it was the new laws that made time feel differently.

Emily opened the door to their homestead and invited Jacque and his family in to relax. What Jacque observed reminded him of his childhood even though there was noticeable change. Ample light emitted from the thin voile curtains around the window that fluttered lightly from the breeze flowing through them and giving the room openness. Jacque also noticed the furniture situated around the room that was new and different, but everything was still a reminder to him of his mother and the past.

"Make yourselves comfortable," Emily and Leona offered. "You remember this house, Jacque, Mama kept us here all of our lives," they reminded.

"And, whenever you ready, you got a homestead," said Leona taking the opportunity to encourage him about the possibility of returning home.

"You're going to see a lot of people that'll give you cause to wonder, but don't worry, some of them are sharecroppers who stayed on the homestead because that's the arrangement. Then, there's our siblings that got family with them; they will be here soon, along with Samuel and Elijah," explained Emily to prepare Jacque for what he could expect.

"There will be celebration tomorrow like you've never seen before on this homestead," Leona added excitedly. Jacque imagined the occasion as he had the day he heard about it and while he was traveling south. He looked forward to the occasion the moment he decided to travel south again, but he remained uncertain about the other siblings.

It took time before Jacque and his family met the other siblings. During their wait, Emily and Leona occupied them with hospitality and made certain they were comfortable. Jacque sat recollecting memories about his life on the homestead and a yearning lingered until he was distracted by his children. They had already gotten used to the environment and were inquisitive. Jacque watched their curiosity emerge.

Viola was prim in her demeanor and Emily and Leona were understanding as they watched in amazement Jacque's daughter who was a mere infant when Jacque left the plantation and who was now an inquisitive young girl examining many of the objects around the room. Viola always made certain that everyone knew she was the first born. Marion listened as she always did to her sister, and looked in the direction of her mother to make certain everything was fine.   Jacque observed his children optimistically thinking how he would not have to describe his origins from a distant land because now his children were in the midst of his birthplace and they would form many impressions that might be recalled in years to come.

Surprisingly, the seething restlessness Jacque always felt being on the plantation had vanished; he felt whole and renewed and looked forward to meeting his siblings. The bright room yielded lavish thoughts and the breeze gave space to the crowded words and memories. The pulling strength of change allowed them to become accustomed to the new appearances, different manners and personalities. Jacque learned some things about Elijah and Samuel he didn't know and Emily and Leona learned some things about Jacque and the north they didn't know. It was like one continuous revelation after another. The vicissitudes of life were apparent and had settled among them, but the Thornton's were bearing through it reacquainting the past with the present. They could have sat there until evening recollecting memories if Emily hadn't caught sight of Samuel and Elijah walking across the field.

Emily and Leona alerted Jacque and his family about their arrival.

"Our siblings are on their way," prompted Emily. We know this won't be easy, but I must tell you, those siblings have regrets.   You'll see for yourself. What Mama said years ago is truth. They're like fallen branches, and if we should see them, don't forget to pick them up."

Samuel and Elijah had anticipated Jacque's arrival at about the same time they could gather the other siblings and join him at the homestead.   They were aware also that time had alienated them and there was a sense of mystery about one more meeting with the past. Of course, with Jacque, it was different. They knew him and it was just a matter of a brotherly relationship thrown asunder coming together again, but the other siblings were different and it would take patience to get through the time lost and hidden judgments.

Jacque reflected upon what his mother had said as he heard his siblings approach. He realized they were not entirely forgotten souls but siblings who compelled him to want to do the same thing – run for freedom. Many nights he lie awake listening in the darkness and walking surreptitiously by the window or door unable to repel the urge to escape. Run for freedom taunted him until he was granted his freedom. The conflict about his siblings persisted. Even though they had run for freedom, they returned to the homestead to rejoin the family. He wasn't certain how he would react when he confronted them.

The trudging of the siblings slowed in front of the house and Jacque caught glimpses of them. It was evident by their appearance they were now men and women with experiences. He could not say he recognized them as siblings or relatives; for the moment, they were strangers. Qualms began to stir in Jacque because he knew his mother's despair about his siblings' disappearance, but at the same time, he understood the yearning for freedom. The contrary emotions and judgments were quickly lashed out before Jacque confronted them. "The truth is still probable," Jacque thought lastly, as his sisters urged him to consider.

"They here," Emily and Leona announced simultaneously. They watched Samuel and Elijah enter the house, while the other siblings remained on the porch.

Jacque immediately recognized Samuel and Elijah and he presumed they recognized him also. There was no hesitation among them to join in reunion.

"Brother," they exclaimed as each moved in a direction to join in kinship and make re-acquaintance. They embraced each other with excitement:

"Is that you?"

"No miles can make brothers strangers."

"The years didn't do nothing but grow our beards and give us wives and children."

"You have come home to a free south, but the Thornton's never believe they were slaves anyway. The Thornton's are a proud family today."

Laughter and conversation spurred the moment. One brother could not utter a word quickly enough before another followed. They knew and understood Jacque's story and he stood verifying some things that had occurred in the north as Elijah and Samuel listened in awe as Jacque abstracted his experiences in the north. He knew they would talk at greater lengths later. Elijah and Samuel related how their lives unfolded on the homestead. Jacque smiled as he heard about their lives as free men leading up to emancipation. Inspired by their togetherness and kinship, they gathered their voices and began to sing as they had many times in the past. They were heard clear across the field and people stopped and listened. Their solidarity was apparent as their dreams and aspirations swirled around them. Jacque, Samuel and Elijah rallied in a bravura far greater than they had ever pursued. The moment was sustained until their voices silenced.

The high-spirited moment finally gave way to the next encounter. Jacque stepped forward to meet his other siblings. Thoughts and memories held conflict as Jacque searched and probed: How should he regard the circumstances? The other siblings understood his uncertainty and dilemma. He could not remember the siblings who had run away. He only saw young shadowy figures without faces. He scrutinized Henry and Ezekiel who were like tall and sturdy statutes, one might see a hundred of them and see something innately familiar, but still he wondered about their kinship as he regarded them. Jacque labored to remember the dark days of he past, but was repelled as painful emotions prevented him. He observed what was before him: three persons claiming to be Thornton's. All of them were silent in their search for discovery. Familiarity did not become apparent to Jacque until he saw Mandolin. In her, he saw resemblance of Emily, Leona and his mother and acceptance of the truth pervaded. The dilemma began to resolve within as the probability of truth asserted. One dark night his siblings had masked themselves to rid the scourge of slavery now the time had arrived to acknowledge who they were.

"All of us been waiting many years to learn about our siblings," Samuel began. "They have returned and say they are Thornton's. We have reason to believe it is true. Now they make re-acquaintance with you, Jacque," said Samuel as he guided them towards Jacque. "This is Henry, Ezekiel and Mandolin, our siblings who run away long ago. The tension was palpable as Jacque was the final one to decide about the siblings. He knew everyone was anxious and Jacque did not keep them waiting any longer. Jacque extended his hands in acceptance and a great sigh of relief was felt among everyone in the room. There were more embraces and laughter and even tears.

***

The following day, surrounded by trees and fair weather, the Thornton's gathered: Jacque, Willa and their three children; Samuel, wife and their two children; Elijah, wife and their two children; Henry, wife and their four children; Ezekiel, wife and their three children; Mandolin and her three children; Emily, Leona and a host of others from the homestead joined in kinship. Freedom enabled them to declare: "We have had experiences and have stood against the seasons and weathered the storms. None of us give up, that's why we're standing here today. We have passed from slaves to free people. Life changes people and makes a new world. We are the generation that marks a new beginning and we will continue believing in our dreams; whatever happens, we can say we stood sturdy like this tree. Faith is shining through today. We welcome our siblings and Jacque, we're grateful you traveled this far and know you can tell us much about what you have seen. Jacque hesitated, but when the words came, his voice was strong and resonant: "This moment brings back a lifetime. Our journey back home reminded me of many things. No longer are we *voices crying in the wilderness*. Our Mama would be happy to know all of her children are here. She always wanted this day to happen. Look at the world, is it not better we stand around this tree to hold the hands that once threw stones in the river to hear the rippling sounds of freedom that have now come together."

Chapter 14

Home Again

In a flash, the auspicious day faded. The ancestors disappeared and the past was gone for the last time. Amalya and J'Nita gazed with sustained wonder and disbelief about what they had experienced. Their silence remained as they hoped other images of the past would appear, but when the stately tree they regarded merely fluttered gently from a breeze, they realized they had already experienced something like impossibility and reluctantly turned from the grand view of the window.

"That's how it happened," Amalya commented finally as she struggled for reality and to reassess the task at hand. She regarded every object around the room with wonder that it might contain some history of their ancestors. Grandma's spirit and vitality pervaded as she considered what must be done.

"We must be diligent," she prompted J'Nita.

"It's all here, isn't it, Mama," J'Nita wondered.

"Grandma wanted us to know about our ancestors, and she provided a way. It's like we ascended a mountain and looked across the world and saw things that we never thought we would. You see, people great and small can make a difference. In every generation there are struggles to overcome. Now it's your generation that will look across the world and have experiences. Be as determined as Grandma and our ancestors were," advised Mrs. Harmon as she returned the journal to the box where it was stored and carefully sealed it. "Whenever we want to revisit the past, we know where to find the journal." They looked through the window once again with yearning and noticed the sun descending and the lateness of the day. They wee immediately prompted and did not delay another second.

Suddenly, they began to race against the clock, diminishing decades' of lingering clutter and items Grandma had amassed: a box there, a book here, linens and clothing, utensils, duplicates of things Grandma used during her lifetime, but could not throw away and stored as keepsakes. They worked without word or interruption. J'Nita maneuvered alongside her mother discarding or arranging everything she contacted. They felt venerated in what they had completed like great historians who portray the last great event that changes the world. The sketchy memories Grandma had recounted had come together like Mrs. Harmon never thought they would. J'Nita didn't know about them as she was in another generation, but Mrs. Harmon marveled in what was manifested within. The revelations burdened her like the elegance of a wedding dress and the memories she carefully searched and wore. How could she forget?

The stored memories were neatly in place and time; the attic transformed to evenly arranged boxes and dressers. In a glance, another dimension appeared about the room: it was now a spacious loft, large, wide and wandering.

"This is the first time I've seen the attic like this, commented J'Nita. "Will we be back tomorrow," she wanted to know. Perhaps the generational probing had already ignited in J'Nita, the kind that ponders for more revelation.

"In another few trips, everything will be completed," said Mrs. Harmon as she surveyed the staid and quiet placement of things. "But, if we don't leave now, your father will be worried."

"Dad is home," J'Nita wondered.

"If those train itineraries ran as scheduled, he should be home now."

They began to gather the items they wanted to carry with them and walked towards the stairs. They walked like on a tightrope deliberately and skillfully. They were careful not to misstep or stumble and let go flying the things they carried with them.

When they reached the bottom of the stairs with everything in tact, they set the cumbersome things down and heaved a sigh of relief. A feeling of bewilderment lingered within them from what they had experienced; the knowledge and lore concerning their ancestors could not readily be forgotten. They walked proudly through the rooms with endearing memories of where Grandma had lived and where family and friends had gathered. They reached the back of the house through the kitchen door leading to the yard. Items lay strewn where they had put them to decide later what they should do with them. They looked at each other with a smile of futility.

"These items have use. In a few days, the Salvation Army will take them away."

J'Nita nodded with understanding and suddenly remembered: "I almost forgot; I must go back to the attic."

"All the way up there again. What for," questioned Mrs. Harmon.

"The cradle," J'Nita replied as she hurriedly left to get it.

As Mrs. Harmon waited, her eyes took inventory of the things that would be taken away: canning items, jars and jugs, she did not have the space for; pots and utensils she had plenty of; blankets and Christmas ornaments, except she noticed a star designed like a snowflake that she decided she wanted. She retrieved it from the pile of items, examined it and found it to be in perfect condition. She smiled in acknowledgment that it would be a useful keepsake. The past would quickly disintegrate, but at least she had memories – the journal – she hesitated … for now, it was safely stored, but on their next trip, she would remove it from the attic and find a place for it in her home.

She was distracted by J'Nita who was awkwardly carrying the cradle. She appeared exuberant that it was now her possession. Mrs. Harmon realized she could not convince J'Nita to leave the cradle in the attic. She offered to help as she saw J'Nita looking strained but determined to carry the item away. Mrs. Harmon grabbed the other side and J'Nita appeared noticeably relieved. "I have an heirloom," J'Nita commented. Mrs. Harmon nodded in agreement as they walked onto the porch. They placed the cradle down while Mrs. Harmon searched for the key to lock the door. It took several moments and it appeared Mrs. Harmon was becoming concerned as to where it was for she had emptied her purse and it did not show up. "Where is it," she questioned aloud.

"Maybe it's in the attic," suggested J'Nita. It now occurred to Mrs. Harmon where the key was. She reached down in her jeans where she had placed it and there it was. "Here," she said as she proceeded to lock the door. She checked to make certain the door was locked before leaving. Again, she assisted J'Nita with the cradle until they reached the trunk of the car where they carefully placed the cradle.

Once in the car, their eyes extended to the darkening horizon and many thoughts recurred about their experiences of the past. They noticed a little desolation of not being where they were earlier. The inextricable bond had outlasted time. On any given day they would remember there is a beginning, an end, a life and history and a day like the one they had experienced which draws everything together like looking skyward, blue crystal clear canvas that has joy, sadness, pulling and tugging and a phenomenal experience of discovery. Mrs. Harmon steered to their destination entirely knowledgeable that all of the times they had traveled the route amounted to the inevitable journey that day.

She steered the car like a cruise down a calm sea, roads winding in smooth sailing across streets and through dark paths with dense forests and rippling water serving up memories. It seemed like a dream, unreal, but believable in its portent – life was simply unpredictable. Who would have thought they would have experienced what they did that day. The day's events were being relieved by both of them. They were thoroughly immersed and didn't seem to mind that they were carried away in time. *A family of love that stays the test of time can last an eternity. The etching of time appeared in a tree; the bough still dripping with promise; the seasons finished with one renewed and the advent of another season....*

A bright light like dawn interrupted their reverie. From a distance they could see their home.

"We're just about home," both of them uttered simultaneously.

"Dad must be there," said J'Nita.

They hadn't seen or communicated with him for days. It was part of their routine and way of life they could not get accustomed. They were never certain when they would see or hear from him.

He had seen them arrive and greeted them with a wave and words that were indistinct, but Mrs. Harmon surmised them to be "Hello," or "Glad you're home." Mrs. Harmon and J'Nita waved back as they got out of the car. They opened the trunk and began to unload some of the items they brought back from Grandma's. Seeing this, Mr. Harmon quickly approached to assist them.

"Shopping always keeps you busy," he commented as he took some items from them.

"Shopping," reiterated Mrs. Harmon, "We've been at Grandma's all this time sorting and organizing things in the house.

"Oh, yes," thought Mr. Harmon silently; the final tasks that must be completed to bring the passing of Grandma to resolution.

"Where do you want me to put these things," he asked as they walked through the door.

Mrs. Harmon thought vacantly as she glanced around the room. Readjusting momentarily, she decided where the items should be placed.

"In the room where Grandma liked to be when she visited," she finally decided.

Her husband was prompted to put the things where Mrs. Harmon suggested, but noticed J'Nita toting what looked like to him an unusual contraption.

"What's that you carrying," he immediately questioned.

"It's a cradle, Dad," she replied anxiously.

"A cradle," he repeated as he stared at it more closely.

"It's a Thornton heirloom and when I was an infant, Grandma used to rock me in this."

"Oh, yeah, I remember now," Mr. Harmon commented with vague recollection. "Where are you putting it?"

"In my room," J'Nita replied proudly.

"I'll help you after I put these things in Grandma's room," offered Mr. Harmon. J'Nita was grateful for her father's help and waited for him to return.

"I must prepare dinner," announced Mrs. Harmon as she walked towards the kitchen.

J'Nita watched her mother until the kitchen light flashed on. She heard her father putting away the items in the room. Her attentions next examined the details of the cradle: round swirl, high back at the head and foot, held together by wide, straight sides and rounded slats at the bottom. Suddenly, the detailing was interrupted by her father lifting the cradle from its position and taking it to J'Nita bedroom.

"Where do you want me to put it," he asked as he entered the room. J'Nita was right behind him and had to first walk around him to see and decide. She noticed a place near the storage bench and she decided that was where it should go.

"Over there," she pointed to let her father know. Her father followed her directive as he thought of the many years that had passed since she was an infant.

J'Nita began to talk incessantly about some of the family history she discovered earlier. By then, they had returned to the sitting room. Her father was a captive listener and J'Nita noticed his compelling interest about what she related.

"Today we learned about our family tree, at least the Thornton side of our family. Mama refers to it as the maternal side."

"Where did I hear that name from," he questioned.

"It's Grandma's side of the family, informed J'Nita.

"That's right," agreed Mr. Harmon as his memory connected.

"Grandma had more family history stored in the house than we could ever have imagined." J'Nita hesitated as she studied her father and decided he was genuinely interested in what she was explaining. She knew that sometimes parents listened with their eyes, but this time it was different.

"We found a journal at Grandma's that dates back to slavery. I didn't have any idea, but no … Suddenly she stopped in the midst of what she was explaining for she realized her father would think she was acting and talking strangely if she mentioned that she had met ancestors and actually saw ancestors from a century ago. How could she explain to him what she had experienced. …

"Is there something to matter," inquired her father noticing her sudden concern.

"There was so much we discovered today, I don't know where to begin," she admitted.

"I understand, and besides you've had a long and trying day."

"But it was phenomenal. If only you were there."

"Well, I can't be in two places at the same time."

"That's it? That's exactly what happened to us today," she exclaimed. We were in the past and the present!"

After the words were uttered, J'Nita realized how incredible they sounded. Her father didn't know what to make of her sudden outburst and didn't consider seriously what the words intended, but he did contemplate an explanation: beginning adolescence, he concluded. The oddity of behavior was evident. He would have to speak to his wife about her and other matters that concerned him. It was now more imperative than ever. Grandma's death proposed the idea. J'Nita was the only child and having other children would be good - one more, maybe two, a boy and a girl, just healthy children. He was set on the idea, but he had to convince his wife. It had been over twelve years since J'Nita was born. The call to dinner interrupted what he was deciding about the future of his family.

At dinner, no conversation was pursued about what had taken place at Grandma's like a cloud had descended around the subject and rendered Amalya and J'Nita speechless. Actually, J'Nita was trying to find the words to explain the day's events at Grandma's as she quietly ate, but was having difficulty. She had not heard a word while her parents discussed the usual items of interest: their friends, the day's events and

213

other matters concerning them. The fascination of the experience preoccupied J'Nita's thoughts. Dinner had concluded before she was able to gather her ideas, leaving unexplained the phenomenal experience she and her mother had earlier.

After dinner, J'Nita remained in the kitchen with her mother, helping where she could and ruminating for explanation. Mrs. Harmon noticed her wavering, but did not question her manner, realizing she was probably tired from a long day and what had occurred. They did not immediately leave the kitchen after they had finished everything, but sat at the table peering at the dark light around the window. The midnight sky was clearly visible, the moon and stars reminded them of the distance they had traveled and how incredible the day had been. Many aspects of the past still remained, memorable impressions that caused them to yearn to be there once again. They lingered until some pulling force made them relinquish their thoughts. Mrs. Harmon left to join her husband and J'Nita went to her room.

When Mrs. Harmon entered the sitting room, she was met by the audible volume from the television and her husband delving into the news of the day. It was post war time and nothing was more complex. The Vietnam war was a difficult one, she nearly lost her husband to re-enlistment, but was glad he decided against it with much urging by her. Protests were still stirring around the country and the veterans were actively visible. Her husband was inherently interested because he was a veteran who served during peacetime and had an honorable discharge. She met him approximately a year after he left the service. They soon married and had J'Nita. That was nearly fourteen years ago. She smiled as she recalled the memories of how she met her husband. Both those thoughts and her husband's commentaries regarding the Vietnam war inundated her.

"The war is over, but the battle is still raging," her husband commented. She had heard the words earlier, prophetic, she thought and then commented: "Are battles really won?"

There was a pause before he replied. When a commercial flashed in place of the news item, a long discussion ensued between them about the issues of the day and the changes taking place. Finally the conversation diverted to where to put the items brought from Grandma's.

"I guess it wasn't easy for you to go over to your Grandma's and tend to matters," Mr. Harmon commented sympathetically.

Once again, she was reminded of what had taken place. Extraordinary, she thought. How could she explain? They had not gotten the chance to discuss what the lost of Grandma meant to them. In fact, they had only indirectly discussed what they would do if anything happened to Grandma. Grandma had been a living testament of longevity and that's all they ever thought about – how long she would live. The void was apparent but together they made their own terms.

As she decided how to finalize the wishes of her grandmother, she studied her husband. He had not changed significantly over the years in her estimation. He had a way of looking forward and going about life with a certain determination. He was still robust and sturdy and continued the regiment of fitness he acquired while in the service. Being over six feet tall, gave him a noticeable physical presence. The days away from home were like an eternity until he returned, but that was the nature of his position at the railway.

"You seem far away," he observed.

I was deciding," said Mrs. Harmon.

"About Grandma's things," he wondered.

"Yes and beyond," she replied. "We had an unusual and trying day. I began to understand Grandma more than ever."

"By sorting through her things," questioned Mr. Harmon.

"It wasn't only that," replied Mrs. Harmon hesitantly. It occurred to her that it was nearly impossible to explain to her husband the experience she and J'Nita had earlier. She now wished her husband had been at Grandma's.

"I know traveling and being away from you and J'Nita have disadvantageous, but it's what I do. Since I returned, I don't know what it is, but it's almost mysterious. It started with J'Nita. She was so overwhelmed, she could hardly talk.

"She was," questioned Mrs. Harmon, knowing there was ample reason for J'Nita's behavior.

"She mentioned something real strange ... like being in two places at the same time – the past and the present. I didn't know what to say."

"Well," said Mrs. Harmon upon realizing the difficulty J'Nita had trying to describe their experience, "It was discovering the cradle that caused her to be so excited. If you can remember, Grandma used to rock her in it. It was stored in the attic all those years and when she saw it, it brought back memories of what took place over the years at Grandma's.

"I understand now, commented Mr. Harmon. "I realized today she's growing to be quite a young lady. She's going through a stage and sometimes it's more obvious than at other times. Adolescence is not the easiest time."

"She is, but she's managing very well. I haven't noticed anything unusual. She's an only child and that can be the difference, explained Mrs. Harmon."

."I'm certain you would have noticed," said Mr. Harmon and simultaneously taking her hand and holding her in his arms in a consoling manner. "I know it will take a while to get over your Grandma." Throughout their relationship, Mrs. Harmon always felt she could depend on her husband for understanding and support. Every fear and sorrow she possessed as a result of Grandma's passing were relieved by Mr. Harmon's consoling manner. Then, in the most delicate manner possible, he began to breach the topic that had been his preoccupation about his family.

"I've been thinking about where all the time has gone. Have you considered J'Nita doesn't have a sister or brother?"

Mrs. Harmon was startled beyond belief about the implications of the words and could only think how incredible they sounded. Many times she had considered what he was alluding to, but the years spent so quickly, the idea – of having other children – became remote. Her mind illuminated with thoughts and suddenly the evening took on an extraordinary and more significant meaning as they nestled together to decide about the future of their family. …

***

In her room, J'Nita sat examining the cradle that reminded her of everything she experienced earlier. "It did happen; I did see my ancestors," she kept reminding herself. Again, she envisioned the images that she saw. She decided to take pencil and paper and write down names in the order she had encountered her ancestors: Mama Thornton, Grandpa John, Emily Thornton, Leona Thornton, Samuel Thornton, Elijah Thornton, Mandolin Thornton, Ezekiel Thornton, Henry Thornton, and a host of other kin to the family she remembered from the journal Grandma left. When she completed each name, she read what she had written. In a voice whisper in the quiet evening, she pronounced: "This is my family – J'Nita's family tree."

THE END